Class No. J   Acc No. C/529750

Author: Carroll - Ann.   Loc: 1 1 MAY 1995

LEABHARLANN
CHONDAE AN CHABHAIN

~~- 8 JUN 1996~~

- 7 OCT 2008

1. This book may be kept three weeks. It is to be
   returned on / before the last date stamped below.
2. A fine of 20p will be charged for every week or
   part of week a book is overdue.

1 AUG 1995	1 5 DEC 2008	
12 OCT 1995	1 2 SEP 2005	
2 6 DEC 1995		
2 7 JAN 1996		
12 FEB 1996		
13 MAR 1996	0 6 MAR 2009	
1 3 MAR 1997		
1 4 JUN 1997		
2 3 SEP 1997		
- 4 AUG 1998		
0 7 NOV 2008		

Rosie's Quest

Rosie's Quest

Ann Carroll

POOLBEG

Published in 1994 by
Poolbeg,
A division of Poolbeg Enterprises Ltd,
Knocksedan House,
123 Baldoyle Industrial Estate,
Dublin 13, Ireland

A catalogue record for this book is available from the British Library.

ISBN 1 85371 281 7

Cover illustration by David Axtell
Cover design by Poolbeg Group Services Ltd
Set by Poolbeg Group Services Ltd in Goudy 11/13
Printed by The Guernsey Press Company Ltd,
Vale, Guernsey, Channel Islands.

For Noel, John & Mary

Chapter 1

"MOM, GRAN'S just flung the cat out of the upstairs window!"

No response.

Rosie McGrath was finding it impossible to get her mother's attention. It was the same every flaming Sunday afternoon! Gran O'Brien would go to bed for a snooze while Mom corrected boring school-work. The red pen would criss-cross over the page while she frowned in concentration. "Oh dear God," she'd sigh, adjusting her reading specs. "Silly Twit-Nit. What a miserable mess." Madge McGrath taught Junior Cert English, a job that caused her deep gloom, especially when she was correcting essays.

"Look at this!" she would almost hiss at Rosie. "The King left the country and was assassinated in his absence. Such twaddle." And she would subside into a furious mutter until another ghastly error caught her eye. Then she'd hold her head in despair and declare, "Rosie, I do not believe this: I gave this imbecile an essay on emigration and what does she write? 'If more people left the country there'd be less emigration'" . . . and so on, for the whole afternoon.

Rosie thought her mother being a teacher was the biggest pain in the world – but then so did her mother!

Madge would moan and groan for hours on end. She'd pull at her hair until it looked like a haystack after a force nine gale. The only comic relief was the contrast between her mother's earnest face and her demented hairstyle.

For the umpteenth time that afternoon she said, "Mom can we go out somewhere?"

Her mother grunted a reply.

Rosie tossed her long fair hair in disgust. Her brown eyes brooded. Obviously, more shock tactics were needed.

"Mom, there's a man in the front garden staring in at us and waving a hatchet."

"That's nice Rosie," Madge murmured. Her daughter got up from the chair in front of the fire, walked across the room and looked out at the cold empty January day.

"Oh look! There's old Mrs Jones on skates and Mr Jones is coming after her on a tricycle!"

Her mother was unmoved by the madness of her elderly neighbours. "Lovely," she declared, obviously paying no attention. "It's wonderful to see old folks enjoying themselves."

Not for the first time, Rosie thought her mother wasn't all there. In fact she was probably a great danger to herself and others. If the house were to blow up on a Sunday afternoon, Madge would very likely continue to correct her copies. Unless of course they went on fire under her nose.

If only I had a sister, Rosie thought. Or even a rotten brother! If only Dad weren't away in Saudi on business for the next three months. He always took her out on Sundays – swimming, bowling, or best of all, over to visit Uncle Jack and his family. They were great fun. Unfortunately they lived miles away on the south side of Dublin. Rosie sighed. If only she and her Mom didn't live in Gran's house. Not that she ever wanted to be without Gran. But it meant living on an old estate, where all the neighbours were elderly, so there was no one for Rosie to play with.

"What I'd really like," she mused, "more than anything in the whole world, is for Aunt Rose to be here. Everything would be different then. I know it would!"

She was quite certain of this, although she could not have said exactly why.

Aunt Rose was her mother's twin, a lawyer living in Boston with her husband Henry and her children Hattie and Shane, also twins. Gran had a letter from her every month, but she never wrote to Mom, which was strange because Mom wrote to her, regularly. Rosie couldn't understand it.

"Oh it's because of the accident your aunt had when she was eleven," Gran said, leaving Rosie more mystified than ever. She knew Aunt Rose had fallen off a swing and cracked her head on the concrete playground. But that didn't explain why she wanted nothing to do with Mom. Unless she'd cracked her brains as well! Though she'd hardly be a successful lawyer if she were insane would she?

"Your Mom will tell you when she's ready," Gran had said when she'd demanded an explanation. But that was ages ago and Mom still hadn't explained. She would fob Rosie off with stories of the twins' first eleven years. Always her eyes would become sad and she would shake her head and grow silent when she came to any mention of the circumstances surrounding the accident.

"You're exactly like her!" She had snapped once when Rosie pressed too hard. "Can't let well enough alone. The same unerring instinct for trouble. Too adventurous and too mischievous by far!"

"I suppose you were a saint," Rosie muttered.

"I was. All teachers are saints. And I was a great comfort to my mother. A perfect child. Whereas you Rosie, keep trying to give me a heart attack with your behaviour."

3

Gran, who had just come in, almost choked.

"Perfect child indeed!" she snorted. "You were as much comfort as a stick of dynamite with the fuse lit. Do you remember that trick you played on poor Mrs Fahy?"

Rosie had been very disappointed when her mother suddenly changed the subject.

Now she pressed her forehead against the window. She would die of curiosity if she couldn't get answers soon. She groaned with frustration and at last Madge looked up.

"What's wrong?" She asked in her soft voice.

"I'm bored," Rosie said crossly, squashing her nose against the pane and watching her breath fan out across the glass.

"Why don't you do something then? Read a book. Watch telly. When I was your age I was never bored."

Well that was hardly surprising! Rosie was indignant. If she'd had a twin sister and a brother like Uncle Jack, she wouldn't be bored either.

"Why are you always correcting every Sunday? I wish Dad were here!"

Madge put down her pen.

"I wish your Dad were here too. And you know why I correct every Sunday. It's because I take you to the pictures every Saturday and this is the only time I've got." She smiled at Rosie. "Anyway, I need a break after that last essay. The daft girl wrote, 'He rowed up the mountain on a donkey. R-o-w-e-d!'" She was outraged. "Can you believe that?" Rosie could. Madge was forever in a state of shock over her students' work.

Some time later she made a cup of tea, Gran came down after her nap and Rosie brought in a plate of biscuits from the kitchen with a glass of coke for herself. They settled cosily around the fire. Munching thoughtfully, Rosie pondered. One thing she couldn't understand.

Eleven year olds didn't fall off swings and nearly kill themselves. Eleven year olds were almost too big for swings. Rosie couldn't stand not knowing any longer.

"Mom, tell me properly about Aunt Rose's accident."

"You know already, not again please!"

"But how come she fell off a swing, Mom? I mean, she was eleven, the same age as me – and I wouldn't fall off a swing!"

Her mother hesitated. But Gran answered for her. Her usually gentle voice was bitter.

"It was no accident!"

Gran's lip was trembling, her kind face pale. Rosie's eyes grew round.

"She was pushed – there's no point in frowning at me Madge, you should tell Rosie exactly what happened and not have the poor child tormented with curiosity."

Rosie was astounded. Pushed! Did Gran mean someone had deliberately tried to kill her Aunt?

Mom answered the unspoken question.

"No it wasn't deliberate. Just a silly game that got out of hand. Your Aunt Rose could never resist a challenge. There was this girl in the class who hated her. Jealous of her really. Rose was so quick and bright and popular and this girl, Agnes Balfe was her name, well, she was big and awkward, a bit of a bully. No one liked her. One day she challenged your aunt to get on the swing and be pushed as high as it would go. Of course Rose couldn't resist. I can still see her laughing . . . She made Agnes Balfe mad. And Agnes pushed harder and harder until the swing was nearly as high as the top bar. And Rose was leaning back, her legs straight out in front of her, smiling as if she were enjoying the whole episode. Then just as the swing reached it's highest point, she let go with one hand to wave to us and toppled over backwards on to the concrete."

Madge's eyes were far away, back in the playground on that long-ago day. Gran was gazing sadly into the fire. Rosie was silent.

"She was in a coma for weeks," Mom went on. "I visited her in hospital once. Her head was wrapped in bandages, her eyes closed. I was sure she was going to die and I couldn't go back. She was there for three months and even though she asked for me over and over I never visited her again and she never forgave me."

"Is that why she doesn't write to you Mom?"

Madge nodded, "When she came home from hospital I thought I could make everything alright; life would be like it was before the accident. But nothing was ever the same again. Oh Rose was polite enough, but she changed her seat in school, took up with different friends – wouldn't go anywhere with me unless she had to.

You know the rest Rosie. When she was seventeen, after the Leaving Cert, she went to stay with your Great Aunt Maura in Boston and studied Law at Harvard and a few years later married your Uncle Henry."

They were silent then, Mom and Gran lost in the past, Rosie thinking how wonderful it would be to meet her cousins.

"It's not fair," she thought "I'll never get to see them." She turned on Madge, "You should have visited her in hospital."

"I know. We'd been together every day since we were born and then when she needed me most I let her down. I was afraid Rosie, I was so sure she'd die. It was impossible to believe she was recovering and I felt if I went to the hospital I'd discover she wasn't alive after all. It wasn't rational. I did try, Rosie. I went back for a second visit but once inside those huge front doors I felt sick and faint, so I had to wait outside on Gran. I don't suppose you can understand."

Rosie didn't, but she knew Mom hadn't meant to hurt

6

Rose and anyway it was all so long ago. Surely her aunt should have gotten over it by now.

"It wasn't just a case of getting over it," Gran explained. "The doctor said the blow to her head could alter her personality. Nowadays they call it 'Post Traumatic Stress'."

Rosie sighed at the waste of it all.

Somehow, even though her aunt had left years before she was born, she'd always felt close to her, as if there were a special bond between them. She couldn't explain it. Maybe it was because they were so alike, as Mom had often pointed out, though rarely as a compliment, more as a telling off.

"Perhaps she's afraid something bad will happen to me too!" Rosie realised suddenly. Aunt Rose was forever playing tricks. Rosie smiled again as she remembered Mom's tales. The details were fixed in her mind as if she'd been there.

Like when the parish priest came to visit. Father Meany. Aunt Rose said his name suited him. Whenever he met a child on the street, he would prod her sharply with his cane and say in a loud voice, "I wonder do we know our catechism today? Can we recite the seven deadly sins?"

If the unfortunate could indeed recite the seven deadly sins, it only served to aggravate Father Meany.

"Oh so we think we know everything," he would sneer, "Well can we explain what Sloth is? Seeing as we're probably such a great example of it!"

If the child faltered at all, Father Meany would keep her there a full ten minutes giving out.

When the priest came to call, it was always tea-time, just when everyone was relaxing. Gran would jump up to do a fry for him, while he tormented the children with his awful questions. "Do we know what Hell is? And what is Calumny?"

7

According to Madge she was the one who always knew the answers, Rose never did and Jack usually managed to wriggle out of trouble.

Anyway, this particular visit was one too many for Rose. It wasn't long after Father Meany had detained her on her way home from school and lectured her for half an hour on Purgatory. After that, Rose said she knew what Hell was like, never mind Purgatory! So when she heard Gran chatting in the hall, some madness entered her soul. Quick as a flash, she took the hard centre out of the best chair and put a cushion there instead. Madge was gobsmacked. Jack choked on his tea.

The door opened and as usual Gran ushered the priest over to the good chair.

"Make yourself nice and comfy there, Father."

So he did.

"Madge, give Father Meany a cup of tea while I fry up something nice for him."

Madge was paralysed, but the cushion held. Nothing happened. Relieved, she handed him the tea.

"And now children," Father Meany sipped. "Do we know what Confirmation does for us?" He smirked as he settled back to listen to the answer. He should never have moved. His bum went through the seat. The cup and saucer flew up in the air and the tea slopped over the floor. Jack snorted. Madge nearly died and Rose – Rose had the cheek to look concerned. Gran came rushing in from the kitchen and couldn't believe her eyes.

Now Father Meany was not a small person. He was a very large man with a very large bum. The more he struggled the deeper he sank. The poor man's knees were nearly in his mouth. Jack lay on the floor and pushed with all his might – in between sniggers. Gran and Madge pulled and tugged at his hands. Rose could do nothing, she was helpless with giggles.

At last he was free – and furious. He snatched his hat and cane and thundered up the hall, Gran following with abject apologies. Granda arrived just as the priest flung by him, muttering indignantly. There was a huge row. Gran called Rose a "brazen hussy" and she was sent to bed early for a week.

Rosie thought her aunt sounded wonderful.

"Are there any old photographs of you and Aunt Rose as children Mom?"

"There were some, but I couldn't bear looking at them after she'd left for America. I'd see her picture and she'd smile out at me just as she used to before the accident. Then I'd remember how she felt towards me, as if I were a total stranger."

"Your Mom was sick for a while after Rose left," Gran added, "and we decided it was better to put all your aunt's childhood things into the attic."

Rosie's heart leapt. So they hadn't thrown anything out. She looked at Gran and Madge pleadingly.

"Do you think I could root around the attic? Take a few of her things? I needn't bring them down here; just keep them in my room. They wouldn't upset you Mom. Gran, could I? Please?"

Mom was uncertain. Gran studied Rosie's serious face and made up her mind.

"Yes of course have a look Rosie! It's time you knew more about your aunt."

Rosie was overjoyed. She could hardly wait now to see Mom going back to her corrections and Gran reading the Sunday papers. Once they were absorbed, she got the large torch out of the garage and made her way upstairs.

It took her only a few minutes to pull down the attic ladder onto the landing. She moved cautiously up the rungs and held her breath as she shone the light around the unfamiliar darkness.

She had come to search for Aunt Rose's childhood, but for some moments she was back in her own past. A doll which could once take a bottle and afterwards pee into a tiny nappy was now lifeless, propped against a beam. ET sat on a broken skateboard, his stuffing knocked out. A remote control robot was hugging a computer game, both long ago broken by their owner.

Rosie moved into the heart of the attic. What exactly did she hope to find? Old photographs, old toys, old books. Gran would have them packed away in some container. In the torchlight, at the far end of the attic, she saw a dusty wooden chest. Clambering over to it she set the light down carefully on a beam and tried the catches. One snapped open quite easily, the other was rusted with age and would not budge. She looked around feverishly for something to break the lock and found an ancient poker. Levering the catch, she gritted her teeth, until suddenly the lid flew up.

Inside was what she had come for – everything that once had belonged to Rose.

Chapter 2

"THIS IS it!" Rosie thought as she shone the torch into the chest. "I know there's something in here I'm meant to find, something that will help me to get Rose and Mom back together, so I've got to look carefully."

Searching through the contents, she came across a jar of glass marbles, an ancient one-armed teddy, a tin of multi-coloured beads, a skipping rope, spinning top, skates with metal wheels and three "William" books. There were old copies – Sums, English and Irish. Not important. Beneath them was a large envelope full of photos. Rosie laid it carefully beside her. Then she found a lovely, small wooden box, with a tiny key still in the lock. The lid was painted with delicate flowers.

These were the treasures to explore.

She sat down gingerly with her back against the chest and pulled out the photographs. Black and white. "The Twins' First Communion Day, 1952" was pencilled on the back of one. Rosie turned it over. Madge and Rose. Sausage ringlets, white dresses, lavish veils, white shoes and socks. The same height but not quite identical. Rose's hair was fairer. Madge was the more serious one, frowning at the camera. Rosie recognised that particular expression – impatient, eager to be elsewhere.

Another photo revealed the twins in "Christmas

Outfits, 1956". Both were glaring at the camera this time. And no wonder! Rosie giggled to herself. They looked like dumpy middle-aged housewives, weighed down in heavy tweed overcoats with velvet collars, topped by bowler hats which made their heads resemble Christmas puddings. In their gloved hands they each held a large handbag. Judging from their expressions the photographer must have been in some danger.

"They're like something out of a comedy act, or characters in a silent movie," Rosie thought.

There were other photos too, most of them not that clear. Distant figures at family picnics, a class full of vague faces. But one close-up showed Aunt Rose, her head slightly to one side, quizzical, staring out of the photograph straight into Rosie's eyes.

"What is she asking me to do?" Rosie wondered, "What can I do after all these years?" She put the picture down.

"I wonder what was kept in here?" Holding the wooden box, she turned the key and lifted the lid. A music box. Unfamiliar notes tinkled sweetly. Inside was a gold heart-shaped locket on a chain. It was beautiful. On one side a single rose was delicately etched, on the other was the inscription: "Rose, Christmas 1956." Mom had a similar locket tucked away in the back of a drawer. Only hers was etched with a daisy – a marguerite. Rosie had never looked inside. Indeed she'd only found it by accident, looking for something else. Mom had been very quick to snatch it and hide it away again.

Rosie opened the locket with a thumb-nail. Two young faces stared out at her. Mom and Aunt Rose in pig-tails with big bows. This time the feeling that Rose wanted to tell her something was overpowering. She traced the small face with a fingertip. How very like her own it was; the same heart shape, small nose and round eyes reaching across the years. Rosie stared intently.

Some old photographs and a locket. It didn't seem much for a whole childhood. There must be more! She closed her eyes.

Then a young girl's voice said very clearly, "I need your help. You must come back." Rosie blinked. She was imagining things.

"Read the diary Rosie, read the diary." The voice was urgent. Then silence. She closed the locket and fastened the chain around her neck.

Seizing the torch, she turned and delved deeper into the chest, under the pile of copies until at last her hand closed around a large book with a clasp. Rosie hauled it out. She had to dust off the cover with her sleeve to make out the faded gold lettering. She held the torch on it and gasped. The inscription read:

Rose O'Brien Secret Diary

1956

This was it! This was the most important find.

Rosie gathered up the photos, the little box and the diary and took them to the comfort of her room.

Sitting on her bed, she laid the treasures on her duvet. She lifted the diary. The clasp was not locked, just a little stiff. It took Rosie a few moments to prise it open. To her surprise, the pages were mostly blank. Not quite two weeks in January were filled in. Then she remembered. Aunt Rose's accident was January 13th 1956. The last entry was for the 12th. There was a page for each day. She decided to start at the very beginning and on the fly leaf she found the following:

> Rose O'Brien
> 20 Innish Road
> Whitehall
> Dublin
> Europe

> The World
> Hite: 4 foot eleven inches
> Hair: Fare
> Eyes: Brown
> Favourite Things: Fry bread, Nancy Balls,
> Gobstoppers, Spangels, Skates, William Books.
> Really Horribil Things: Boys (except Jack and
> William), Tripe, Semolina, Senna (yuck).
> Really Horribil Persins: Miss Hackett, Aggie Balfe
> and Mrs O' Kelly.

Rosie smiled. The spelling was desperate. Yet she had seen one or two of her aunt's typed letters to Gran and hadn't noticed any mistakes.

Maybe that blow to her head turned her into a good speller, Rosie mused. I wonder what senna is? And Nancy Balls sound a bit rude whatever they are.

As for semolina! Gran had once given her some. Rosie thought it looked like sick that had been put into a blender.

"Do I eat this, or have I eaten it already?" she'd asked rather too smartly. Mom had made her swallow every bit of it and do all the washing up afterwards.

Maybe the diary would reveal who Miss Hackett was and Mrs O'Kelly. She already knew about Agnes Balfe. She turned to the first day of 1956. Under Sunday 1st, Rose had written:

> My New Year's Resolushons are to:
> 1. Make a Gobstopper last two hours
> 2. Become a tite-rope walker
> 3. Help Madge aggrevate Mrs O'Kelly
> 4. Wallip Aggie Balfe
> 5. Pray Miss Hackett will give up teachin' and become a Belly dancer in Turkey.

Rosie smiled. For a moment she imagined her own teacher, Mr O'Gorman (fondly known as Stormin' Norman) learning to belly dance. His double-glazed glasses glinting over a yashmak as he swayed in a flimsy skirt and size fourteen boots to Turkish music. Well, maybe not.

In the first week of 1956, the O'Brien children were still on holidays and having a great time, as Aunt Rose recorded in her unique way.

Monday 2nd: It must of snowed all night. Me and Madge and Jack made a snow woman after breakfast. It should of been a snowman but Dad took back his cap an pipe an specs. So we used Ma's old nightie an a swimmin' cap. Jack wanted to put a pair of Ma's nickers on the snow woman's head, but I knew that would make Ma cross. She woudn't want the neyburs to see her nickers treated disrespeckful. She woudn't want the neyburs to see her nickers at all. In the afternoon we sneaked out buckets of water to make a slide on the path while Ma was lissenin' to *Mrs Dale's Diary*.

Tuesday 3rd: Mrs Fattie an the postman an Rover next door fell on top of one another on our slide. Rover licked Mrs Fattie's face and she whacked him with her handbag. So Rover bit the postman. Madge and me very kindly offered our help. I says, "Can we assist you to get up Mrs Fattie?" She tried to hit me with her handbag. "My name is Mrs F-a-h-y," she says, sitting on the slide. She must of damidged her brain when she fell. Her hat was knocked over one eye. "Just gimme your hand, Mrs F-a-h-y," I says, tryin' to be nice. She wouldn't an' we couldn't help the postman 'cos he was still strugglin' with Rover. When they did get up evenchooly they gave out stink an told Ma. We had to throw clay on the slide an' Ma took her nightie off the snow woman. It looked silly with only a swimmin' cap on.

Wednesday 4th: The snow is melting an' our snow woman is only a blob wearing a swimmin' cap. Jack decided he would help Madge and me become tite-rope walkers. Under his eggsellent manidgement we woud learn to cartwheel an hop on the tite-rope an be known as Marvelluss Madge an Ramblin' Rose. I thought Ramblin' Rose sounded like a loonatick but Jack says you have to have a word starting with the same letter as your name if you want to be a great arteest.

He tied one end of the rope to the top of our railins an the other end to the top of Morans' railins across the road. I stepped on the rope an fell off immeejitly. Marvelluss Madge manidged about four steps. The Reilly's came out to join in. They were hopeless. Jack says we're all useless an' Eustiss Reilly is the uselessest 'cos he got tangelled in the rope. He said his profeshnal advice was we should forget about tite-rope walking an' become slack-rope walkers – just put the rope on the ground an' walk on it. Ha Ha Very funny, I don't think!

Thursday 5th: It rained all day an' nothing happened. I read *William the Outlaw* an' played Dominoes an' lissened to *Children's Hour*. All the snow is gone.

Friday 6th: Madge an' me an Jack went to ten o'clock Mass except Jack was late. Father Meany spied him from the altar an' said,] "That boy is late. He should apollygise to the Lord." "Sorry Father," says Jack. He was beetroot. Father Meany was miffed. "Apollygise to the Lord boy, not to me!" he shouted. Jack got redder. "Oh sorry, Father," he says again. He couldn't help hisself an' Father Meany was glaring. Madge and me had to leave Mass twice 'cos we were laffin' so much.

Saturday 7th: Second last day of freedom. Me an' Madge an' Linda Reilly went to the Drum to see *Calamity Jane*. Smashin' picture. Jack and Eustiss Reilly went too an' sat with their pals. We pretended the bus home was the Deadwood Stage Coach. We had a gun fight with Jack an' Eustiss but Jack always has to eggsaggerate. When Madge shot him he fell slowly into the middle of the bus an' was dead for five minutes. He is not a normul persin.

Sunday 8th: Last day of freedom. Horribil Miss Hackett an' more horribil Aggie the Haggie. Went to the museum of Nacherel History with Dad and Madge. I thought the gorilla looked like our Jack except Jack is much more life-like. Ha Ha.

Aunt Rose must have been great fun, thought Rosie. No wonder Mom still misses her. That first week of 1956 had something magical about it. The tight-rope walking, the snow woman, the Reilly children, all grown up now and gone away. The diary, full of life and laughter, made Rosie sad. She read on . . .

Monday 9th: Back to school to Miss Hackett's Torcher Chamber, what she calls Fifth Class. Agnes Balfe walliped me at dinner time. During singin' Miss Hackett told me an' Madge to "utter not another note" an' fined us a penny for the Black Babies 'cos our singin' was dyabolikal! I thought we were very mellojuss. She said Agnes Balfe on the other hand sang like a bird. "A crow! A vulcher! A baldy headed eagle!" I whispered to Madge. Aggie heard me. She tried to knock me over. I ignored her. Here is a good joke. What do you get if you cross a vulcher with a budgie? You get a bird that goes C H E E P! (You have to really roar C H E E P!)

Tuesday 10th: A Sums test! Miss Hackett said whoever came last would have to wear the Donkey's Tail. Lucky I am good at sums. Agnes Balfe said a Donkey's Tail would suit me. I told her she would never look like a donkey an she looked pleased until I added "Just a elefant." She promised to get me. She really has a terribil temper.

Wednesday 11th: Saw Mrs O'Kelly on the way to school an Madge roared a really rudie rhyme at her an raced around the corner to hide, with me followin'. I think Mrs O'Kelly saw us. Agnes Balfe dared me to take up the High Swing Challenge an' Madge told her to scram but I said I would if she would. That shook her. Then I said I'd fight her instead. She was thrilled 'cos she thought she'd beat me. But I walliped her. Madge was proud. I have a bad feeling about it though.

      Tonight Da brought us to the pantomime in the Royal. It was Brillo.

Thursday 12th: I knew when I saw Mrs O'Kelly comin' into the class it meant trouble. She was glarin' at us. In her best prissy-sissy voice she goes, "I hate to interrupt your class Miss Hackett, but the deploribil behaviour of the O'Brien twins makes it nessessry. They disgraced me on the way to school this morning with their rude and nasty yellin'. A poor man passin' on his bike nearly fell off with the shock."

      Madge tried to take the blame an I encouridged her. But it was no good. We were given six of the best an put in the Dunces' row. That Madge is a real troublemaker.

      I have just realised that tomorrow is Friday the Thirteenth. I keep thinkin' something awful will happen! Maybe I'm just imagining things. Daft!

That was her aunt's last entry. Rosie closed the diary. She sat staring into space as the evening darkened. Now she knew who Miss Hackett was and guessed Mrs O'Kelly was some other teacher. But why did Madge dislike her? Rosie had learned a little, not only about her aunt but also about Mom. Mom the tight-rope walker. Mom the yeller of rudie rhymes! Rosie giggled.

She thought again of her aunt's call for help, "You must come back." Perhaps Rose was as unhappy as Madge, caught in a time warp she didn't know how to escape. Perhaps the adult Rose didn't even realise she wanted life to be different; to change the consequences of that stupid accident. But the girl in the photograph knew. Rosie closed her eyes. The shadows in the room deepened. "I wish you were here Aunt Rose," she said intensely, over and over, like a prayer. Somehow she would find a way to change the past, to bring Mom and Aunt Rose together again.

Then she heard Gran's voice calling her for the evening meal.

Chapter 3

ON MONDAY morning Rosie sat at the breakfast table half asleep. Her eyelids drooped and her spoon stopped in mid-air. She nodded off and her face collapsed gently into the cereal bowl.

"Rosie!" The spoon clattered to the floor and she jerked her head up, shocked into waking. Milk streamed down from her forehead, dotted with the odd Rice Crispie. Gran chuckled, dabbing at her with a tea towel. Mom groaned, "Stop dozing Rosie. Hurry up and I'll give you a lift."

Rosie muttered. "Oh no! Now I'll be really late."

She packed away her lunch: peanut butter sandwiches, prawn cocktail crisps, toffees, pineapple yoghurt, a raspberry milkshake and some chocolate fingers.

"Enough to feed the whole class," Madge complained. But Rosie believed there would be no point in going to school at all if she didn't have something good to eat at break. She checked her pocket for her bag of chewing gums. Mom hated the stuff.

"It gives you a sneering expression," she said, "makes you look tough, as if you couldn't care less about anything." Rosie was delighted. All that for ten pence!

As usual she was ready before her mother, who always made at least four trips to the car before setting off. Now

Rosie stood in the porch glancing impatiently at her digital calculator watch. Stormin' Norman got very upset if anyone was late and was immune to all excuses.

"I slept it out," made him gnash his teeth.

"The dog died and I had to bury it," Rosie had tried once.

"You don't have a dog Rosie," he'd retorted.

"It wasn't my dog, it was someone else's, Sir."

"Feeble bluster," he'd said. "Three page essay tonight. 'My Imaginary Dog.'"

Waiting patiently she listened to Sinéad O'Connor on her Walkman.

"Can I get my head shaved and wear eighteen hole Doc Martens?" She'd asked her mother.

"No. I will not have a baldy eleven year old daughter tramping around in corner boy boots. Next thing you'll want to paint your scalp purple and wear a safety pin in your nose."

Mom could be so unreasonable.

Suddenly the earplugs were whipped away and Madge was shouting, "For God's sake stop loitering. We're late as it is." Rosie was indignant. Who had been ready for ages?

"I hate school," she muttered as she climbed into the back of the car. "I hate Monday mornings." Her voice rose. "I have eight years of school left! Another eight years of flamin' Monday mornings!"

This was not the thing to say to Madge who had no desire to go to school either.

"Eight years is it?" she snarled. "Well I'll have you know I have been at school, some sort of school – primary. secondary, college – for over forty years Rosie. Over forty years! Ever since I was four. No one wants to go to school for that long. Not even a teacher! And I have another twenty to go. So I'll have spent sixty odd years in school before I'm finished. And very odd some of them were! You don't know how lucky you are. Don't whine to me about a piffling eight years!"

"Why don't you leave then?" Rosie muttered, but only to herself. She couldn't get a word in edgeways and anyway the last time she'd asked that question, it had been answered in such detail Rosie couldn't follow the half of it and had nearly died of boredom. It was something to do with Mom being in the house all day and occupying her mind while Dad was away.

Madge could not be stopped. She gave out all the way, turning around to glare at Rosie. Tyres screeched and horns honked as she veered to the opposite side of the road. Rosie was petrified. Why had she opened her mouth? Now Mom was onto her favourite theme.

"The trouble with you is you get too easily bored! Always looking for excitement. Imagine tying Mr O'Gorman's shoelaces together under the table! Just like your Aunt Rose! A born trouble-maker."

Rosie thought of the last entry in the diary and wisely said nothing. Any mention of rudie rhymes and a murky past might lead to a car crash. She heaved a sigh of relief when at last they arrived. One thing worse than Sunday afternoons, worse than any Monday morning, was Mom's driving.

But as she said good-bye, she noticed Madge's eyes were sad.

She's thinking about Aunt Rose again, Rosie knew at once. She pondered: I bet twins feel like one person. After all, they share practically everything – clothes, toys, friends. They're in the same class and do everything together. Rosie wandered into the schoolyard, still working it out. I suppose it must be worse than anything for twins to break up, like losing a part of themselves.

No wonder Mom got sad. And not Dad or Gran or Rosie could fill the empty space.

I have to do something. I have to get Aunt Rose back. But how? How?

"Hurry Rosie. The bell went three minutes ago."

It was her school friend Helena, charging past her to beat the teacher into class. Monday had begun in earnest.

"Quick march. In your desks. English book out. Page ten. Revise spelling." The orders were barked out. He stood tall and commanding by his table. Not for nothing was his nickname Stormin' Norman. The classroom was his battlefield and he was a five star general. Sometimes he saw the children as recruits, learning the necessary lessons for survival. Other times they were the enemy, forced to surrender to his superior strength. On a Monday they were definitely the enemy.

"Guess what I found yesterday in the attic?" Rosie whispered to Helena. Next second Stormin' Norman was at her side. Arms folded, glasses glinting, he stood over her.

"No talking. One warning. Lines next. Revise Please. First to be asked." And off he marched. He talked like a machine gun. It didn't do to upset him, especially on Mondays when he was as prickly as the rest of the class.

Rosie was lucky. She was a good speller and didn't miss a word. Then just as she was breathing easily again and settling down for a snooze while the rest of the class suffered on, Stormin' Norman tapped the pile of copies in front of him.

"Essays," he said and stared ominously at Rosie.

"Oh no!" she groaned.

As he handed each one back his eyes remained fixed on hers. "Anthony McElheron: Brilliant story. Set in India. 90%.

Peggy McNulty: Badly planned. Mix-up in the months of the year. 60%.

Susan Mansworth: Nice title. 'My Wonderful Mom.'

23

Story less good. Mother spends two pages hanging out washing! 30 %.

Rosie McGrath: Extraordinary." He paused, holding her copybook distastefully as if it had some horrible disease.

Rosie's heart sank. She knew exactly what he meant by "extraordinary" and it wasn't "brilliant" or "excellent." On Friday afternoon he had given them an hour to write a three page essay of their choice. She'd managed a long paragraph. Well, it was Friday and she had other things to think about – like football after school and the films next day. Now she was truly sorry.

Stormin' Norman looked at her over the top of his specs. He read:

The Rotten Tooth
by DKN Amill

Molar was the rottenest tooth in the whole world. He gave his owner – a sweet girl called Tootsy – a big big pain in the face. He filled the air with a foul and horrible smell. It reminded people of stinking socks. So Tootsy had no friends. All her family wore filter masks. One day she went to the dentist. Her heart would have been in her mouth from fear but it couldn't stand the smell. She sat back in the dentist's chair. "Open wide," he said. She did. He fainted. But he was a brave man and fought tooth and nail to help her. Wearing an oxygen mask, he went to work. "Cracked it!" he said, holding up Molar in two halves . . .
The End.

The class was giggling but Stormin' Norman shook his head. "Short. Lack of effort. Plenty of imagination. Do better. Tonight. Three pages. Same title."

Rosie groaned. A typical start to the week. Maybe a

chewing gum would cheer her up. Carefully her hand went
to her skirt pocket and eased two round gums out of the
bag. One she passed to Helena. Then she put her elbow on
the table and her hand over her mouth and gazed
innocently at the teacher as he continued with the essays.
The gum slipped into her mouth with ease. After years of
practice she could keep her face still while her tongue
sucked and tasted – except she had forgotten it was sour
ball which promised to "bring tears to the eyes with its
unique acid taste." Her expression changed and Helena
was gasping.

Stormin' Norman was down at once.

"Dreadful girl. Eating again. Hand it over!" He
snatched the bag.

Now it was Stormin' Norman's policy whenever he
confiscated sweets, to sit at his table and slowly and
deliberately eat them in front of his pupils. This policy
worked, he'd once told them, because it was so darned
mean! No child, he explained, could bear to see a
miserable teacher enjoy the sweets they'd bought with
their pocket money. And of course, it hurt him a lot more
than it hurt them!

Just how true this was he'd soon discover. Rosie
quaked. Without even looking at the bag Stormin'
Norman took a red sourball and popped it into his mouth
calmly and triumphantly. He sucked vigorously to show
Rosie just how much he was enjoying her sweet. Helena
gripped her arm, aghast.

For a moment nothing happened. Then Stormin'
Norman blinked, once, twice, rapidly. His eyes watered
and his mouth twisted into a puckering prune. His face
grew red and sweaty. The class was mesmerised. He drew
out a hanky and spat the chewing gum into it.

"Y a a g h!" he bellowed. His pupils sat terrified. Only
Rosie and Helena knew what he'd eaten. The rest thought

he was poisoned. He thought so himself.

"Vile stuff. Vile person. What was it? Explain girl."

"Chewing gum, Sir. Sourball. It's lovely. You should have bitten into it, then . . . "

"Instant death. Like liquid acid drops. Pint of vinegar. Dreadful experience."

He mopped his brow with his hanky and the chewing gum stuck to his forehead.

"Oh no," moaned Rosie. Her class-mates had no such worries. Their teacher wasn't going to die on the spot. This made them light-headed after the panic he'd caused. They began to titter, staring at the red ball stuck to his forehead like a misplaced clown's nose. They became hysterical. Helena got a pain from laughing and had to stand up, clutching her side. He shook his head in disbelief and the gum dropped to the ground. Slowly the mirth subsided, giving way to the odd hoot, the odd hiccup.

"Most amusing." There was a dangerous glint in his eye. He saw Rosie's despairing face, then looked at the bag and saw the description.

"Should have read this first. No more chewing gum, Rosie!"

"No Sir, definitely not Sir."

She heaved a great sigh of relief. She could have sworn she saw a faint smile on Stormin' Norman's face. Which was why, when she was asked to read aloud a short time later, she risked her life again. It took only a glance to see the first paragraph was full of R's.

"Gweat," she said to herself. "Widdled with aws. Today I can't pwonounce aws." Rosie loved living dangerously. She began:

"*Willie to the Wescue* by Wonald Wushton. Willie wode acwoss the wange on his woan horse to wescue his best fweind Wusty from mudewous cowboys. They had twapped him and his Pawwot Pwetty Polly in the gwim shack and were shooting fuwiously at them. Willie could hear the pawwot scweeching 'Pwetty Polly wants a dwink,' while Wusty was woawing, 'Huwwy Willie! Huwwy to the wescue.'"

By the time Rosie had finished the first sentence, the class was in fits. Hands were stuffed into mouths to stifle giggles. Yet Stormin' Norman didn't stop her. He seemed to be staring intently at a speck on the ceiling. Odd sounds came from his direction and he was overcome by a sudden fit of coughing. Rosie's voice began to waver. Then the bell went for small break and Stormin' Norman brusquely waved the class out.

"I don't know where you get the nerve Rosie," Helena said admiringly, as they tucked into their milkshakes and biscuits. "You'd better not do anything else or he'll explode."

"You're right. I'll be a model person for the rest of the day."

"I hope you have your new Science copy then. He's starting today and he warned us on Friday."

It was obvious from Rosie's face she hadn't got the copy.

"Rosie he'll murder you. He'll leave fingerprints around your neck!"

This was one of Stormin' Norman favourite threats and now it just might happen.

Rosie had to get that Science copy. If she raced round to the shops she could manage it in time.

"I have something really exciting to tell you about my aunt, but it'll have to wait."

She rushed off, leaving Helena aghast. No one was allowed to leave school at small break. Rosie would be suspended if she was caught. On the other hand, if she didn't have her Science copy . . .

27

Rosie bought it in record time. On her way back she began to think of Aunt Rose. If wishing would help, she would wish again and again her aunt were back home with Mom. As she ran, the words drummed in her mind, keeping pace with her pounding feet.

"I wish things were different – I wish you were here. I wish things were different – I wish you were here."

All her thoughts were focussed on those words, so that crossing the road, she did not see the speeding car. Only felt its glancing blow as she was knocked onto the kerb.

Chapter 4

ROSIE SWIRLED downwards into a tunnel; a blackness so dense it could have been a thousand feet beneath the earth. Absolute silence. She stayed still, waiting for her eyes to adjust. But she could see nothing. Her mind was incapable of thought. In the distance a gap of light appeared and widened, like a shutter moving across a lens. Automatically she stepped towards it.

It never occurred to her, not even for a moment, to turn round and go back. Steadily she advanced towards what seemed to be sunlight at the end of the tunnel.

She was nearly at the opening when a shadow brushed past and a small voice whispered, "Thank you Rosie and good luck." The figure was hazy, barely heavier than the air. It moved back the way Rosie had come. She felt no urge to turn and watch, only an irresistible longing to reach the light. She stepped outside the tunnel and at once the sunlight dazzled her and her mind reeled again.

When she came to, she sat up blinking. The speeding car was long gone. She felt a large lump at the back of her head but there was no blood.

"I must have been knocked out and that creep of a driver didn't even stop." Gingerly she got to her feet. No bones broken, just a little stiffness. This time she looked left and right before crossing. But there wasn't a car to be seen.

"Weird. I could've sworn there were loads of parked cars. The drivers must have seen me when they moved off. So why did nobody help?"

But there was no time to think further. If she didn't go in at once, Stormin' Norman would strangle her. The schoolyard was deserted and when Rosie looked at her watch, she realised she was very late indeed.

"Where's my blasted Science copy? I must have left it lying on the path! Too late to go back now."

The corridors were empty and she could hear the murmur of teachers and children in classrooms. Yet suddenly Rosie was afraid. Worse still, she felt certain she was in an unknown place. Something wasn't right – but what?

"Probably my head. Mom always says it's not screwed on properly. That blow must've loosened my brain. Where else could I be except outside good old Fifth Class?" She smiled and opened the door.

"Come in here at once girl and stop dawdling. That's the last time you get permission to go out to the toilet." A harsh female voice greeted her. Rosie stood in the doorway, confounded. It was her classroom alright, yet completely different. The room was packed with girls wearing strange clothes. And the frowning teacher was certainly not Stormin' Norman. She was. She was. Miss Hackett. Miss Hackett! The words screamed into Rosie's brain.

Miss Hackett stood at her desk on a raised platform. Her hair was scraped back into a bun. A long drooping nose met an aggressive chin. With no effort at all Rosie could imagine a pointy cone-shaped hat on her head and a broomstick in her hand.

Miss Hackett stamped her foot, "Close that door at once and stop staring. Go and sit beside your sister immediately if you don't want a slap." She cut a menacing swish through the air with a bamboo cane. In the front desk by the window was an empty space and Rosie hastily made for it.

She felt dazed. Everything was very odd. No group tables. No artwork. No goldfish or plants. No bookshelves or colourful notice board. Just cold blue walls and a picture of the Sacred Heart over the blackboard. Two huge statues of angels stood on either side of it. One was gazing at the ceiling with a gormless smile while the other was doing his best to squash a snake under his foot. His eyes were fierce. Rosie's sympathies were with the snake. It was no joke having a two ton angel stamping on you.

She took in the rows of desks. What an amazing number of girls! Fifty-six altogether. And all so quiet. No boys either. It was weird!

Stormin' Norman thought thirty-eight pupils were far too many.

"Disgraceful number," he would explain, "Disaster. Turn out hooligans."

As she stared, fascinated, Rosie got a sudden dig in the ribs and her companion whispered, "Miss Hackett is watching you Rose, look at your book." She did so. Not that she could make much sense of the words in front of her. She listened to the girl reading aloud. Irish. Yet the page in front of her had spots all over it, on top of various letters. Spotty Gaelic. Mega weird!

She sneaked a look at her companion and almost gave a shout. Mom! Aged eleven. She recognised her instantly from Rose's locket. "What are you gawking at?" her refined mother hissed fiercely. "Would you look at your dratted book, you'll have us both in trouble." Rosie looked down. All of a sudden she noticed her clothes.

Oh no! What kind of gear is this? It's disgusting. In fact she was the same as every one else. Hideous. Wearing a black gym-slip with a green sash around the waist. Wide pleats made her chest look like a balloon. Underneath was a blouse and a green jumper. Around her neck was some sort of horrible knitted tie. The socks were brown and thick and ribbed and turned down at the knees. And whatever she was wearing underneath her uniform felt very bulky indeed.

She explored cautiously. Aaaagh! Long thick heavy knickers! With elastic just above the knee. She shook her head in disbelief and felt two heavy weights – plaits – tied with disgusting bright green ribbons. Yuck!

"Sums!" Miss Hackett shouted from the top of the class. Irish books were closed with one accord. In total silence desks were lifted and Sums copies taken out. A vicious dig from Mom told Rosie to do the same. She wasn't really surprised to find her aunt's name on the front of her copy.

"Now. Let's go over some very simple things first, in case anyone has forgotten them during Christmas. You, Rose O'Brien. We all know you're a genius at mental arithmetic, so do inform us how many pennies there are in a pound?"

The class giggled politely. One of Miss Hackett's little jokes. It was dangerous not to show appreciation. Anyway Rose O'Brien was good at Sums and this was a simple question. Even the girls in the Dunces row knew the answer – which was why they nearly fell off their chairs when Rosie said, "One hundred, Miss."

Beside her Mom groaned. The girl in front gave a nervous shout of laughter.

"Fool!" said Miss Hackett, "And stand up at once! How dare you stay sitting down to answer." Her face was becoming an interesting shade of purple.

"The answer is two hundred and forty, Miss" said Mom quickly. Miss Hackett glared at Rosie, then turned to the board and wrote:

	L	S	D
Twenty pence	=	1	8
Thirty pence	=	2	6
Forty pence	=	3	4
Fifty pence	=	4	2
Sixty pence	=	5	0
Seventy pence	=	5	10
Eighty pence	=	6	8
Ninety pence	=	7	6
One hundred pence	=	8	4

Rosie couldn't make head nor tail of it. It's old money, she realised. Imagine having to learn this. Poor Mom. Poor Aunt Rose. Then the awful truth hit her with full force. I'm sitting beside my Mom. Only she's not. Not yet. She's Madge O'Brien . . . and I've taken Aunt Rose's place. Everyone thinks I'm Rose O'Brien! Her mind was about to grapple with the full meaning of this when Miss Hackett interrupted.

"Now Rose O'Brien. Tell the class please what the answer is when you subtract seven and six from eight and four." Rosie bit her lip. Seven and six was thirteen, eight and four was twelve. Take thirteen from twelve. Can't be done. Must be the other way round.

"The answer is one, Miss."

There was a hastily smothered giggle. A large girl in the next row put up her hand.

"Yes Agnes, you tell this stupid girl what the answer is!"

"Ten pence, Miss," came the triumphant reply.

"Thank you, Agnes, we can always depend on you."

So this was Agnes Balfe. A large girl, she looked older than the others. Glancing over at Rosie, she smiled unpleasantly and wiped her nose on her sleeve. Her hands were large and raw. Her fringe was slicked into three large

33

commas and the hair on the top of her head escaped from the rest to stand up in wild tufts. She had very fine hair.

"She looks like a tough overgrown baby," Rosie thought and smiled at the image. Agnes Balfe scowled at her and suddenly there was nothing babyish about her.

"Now Rose O'Brien," Miss Hackett was standing on her platform tapping her cane thoughtfully, "I've a good mind to give you six of the best for your tomfoolery. However, as I'm giving the class a Sums test tomorrow, I'll wait 'til then."

There was a general groan. Just back from Christmas holidays to face a Sums test!

"Silence," roared Miss Hackett, "I will not tolerate mutiny. Tomorrow you will do a test on shop bills and anyone who does not pass will wear the Donkey's Tail. Is that clear?"

Depressed silence filled the class room.

"Is that clear?" And Miss Hackett cut through the air savagely with her cane. Her nose seemed to touch her chin.

"Yes Miss Hackett," they gabbled.

She pointed at the board. "It will stand to each girl here to know these money-tables off by heart. Know them like you know your prayers and you'll remember them forever. Now girls, what is my motto?"

"Tables is for life, Miss."

"*Are* not *Is*."

What a load of rubbish! Rosie thought. A fat lot of use those tables will be in another few years. "Tables is Torture" should be the motto. Miss Hackett is flamin' torture. You'd think she was running a prison for dangerous criminals.

Rosie remembered Stormin' Norman with sudden fondness. He would never call anyone stupid or a fool and he didn't need a cane. He was like a cuddly teddy bear compared to this teacher. But Miss Hackett had not forgotten her.

"And now Rose O'Brien, let's get back to absolute basics since you seem to have forgotten everything you ever learned. How many fartings in a half crown?"

Fartings? Rosie couldn't believe her ears. "I don't understand the question Miss," she said desperately. She felt quite unable to discuss farting with Miss Hackett. Even if it was the name of an old coin. Really she wasn't a bit surprised the government had changed the money. It must've saved a lot of embarrassment all round.

The rest of the class waited expectantly. What was Rose up to? Pretending not to know this baby stuff.

Miss Hackett was furious. "Of course you understand! Don't you play the fool with me Miss."

"But I don't know what fartings are," she wailed. She didn't know much about half crowns either, but they hadn't captured her attention in the same way.

The class was so appalled at this piece of outrage they forgot to laugh. Miss Hackett would kill her. The teacher stared at her, her face pale. But the girl's confusion was obvious and Miss Hackett narrowed her eyes. It wasn't possible the child was mocking her.

At last she broke the silence. "I said 'farthings'." Her tone was mild enough. "If you had a titter of wit Rose O'Brien, you'd have realised that. One day you will go too far."

She was saved by the bell, for just then the Angelus rang out. The girls stood immediately and blessed themselves while Miss Hackett began the prayer. Rosie knew none of the responses, but she mumbled well enough, keeping her head bowed and her hands joined. She sneaked a glance at the other row. Agnes Balfe looked very holy altogether. Eyes closed, head sunk, saying the words as loudly as possible. At the 'Amen' she raised her head and caught Rosie's half smile. She flushed deeply.

"Five minutes for meditation girls." They sat down. Rosie meditated on how she would escape from this weird world and save Aunt Rose. Idly she picked up a pencil and began to doodle on the back of her copy. What was she to do about Agnes Balfe? It was clear the girl disliked her aunt from the way she'd answered the sum and from the filthy look she'd just thrown at Rosie.

"Ouch!"

A hot pain seared through her as the bamboo cane swished down on the back of her hand. It swooped again. Rosie cried out in hurt and outrage. Tears spilled. She nursed her injured hand, rocking backwards and forwards.

"How dare you. How dare you sit and draw when you have been told to meditate. I will tell you when you may draw! Give me that copy."

Miss Hackett snatched it and looked at the back cover. As Rosie had not much talent for art, it was not a good picture. And it wasn't at all complimentary to Agnes Balfe. Yet she had managed to capture something of the girl's spiteful look. Although Agnes had all her teeth, Rosie had drawn only the one that stuck out.

Miss Hackett showed the picture to the class. She walked up and down the rows so that each child could see it. At Agnes Balfe's desk she paused and handed her the copy.

"Tear it up dear." The girl looked at the drawing and seemed to swell with rage. She ripped the copy to shreds.

"Now give it back to Rose O'Brien"

She lumbered out of her seat, over to Rosie, flinging shreds of paper at her.

"You'll be sorry for this you mean little tramp!"

Rosie did feel mean. She hadn't really known what she was drawing and certainly wouldn't have shown it to the whole class. No wonder Agnes Balfe was upset. But imagine telling her to tear up the copy!

Her class mates were delighted with the drama and were firmly on Rose O'Brien's side. They had all suffered at the hands of Agnes Balfe who, finding she was not liked, had opted for being hated instead. She was famous for twisting arms, and biting ears and kicking viciously. What she called her "Super Strategy" was the worst. She would take a run at an unsuspecting victim and bowl them over by sheer force of weight. Many girls went home with bloodied hands and knees and bruised, scraped faces after such an attack. So there was no sympathy now for her humiliation. The big girl sensed this and it enraged her even more.

A gong echoed loudly through the school.

"Dinnertime thank Heavens!" Madge whispered. "We'd better run home as fast as we can. Agnes Balfe is looking at you."

Rosie followed Madge swiftly to the cloakroom. She took down a similar coat and recognised it as part of "'Christmas Outfit, 1956'." She pulled gloves and a hat from her pocket and stalled over the hat. It was truly horrible. A sort of knitted bonnet that fastened under the chin. But Madge, clearly in a panic, urged her to hurry. They rushed off while Agnes Balfe was still buttoning her coat.

"Hey you two!" The enemy was not so easily evaded. "I'm going to batter you, Rose O'Brien. You're minced meat!" She thundered down the corridor after them, catching up as they tried to jostle their way through the crowd surging out the door. Manoeuvering herself in front of them, she waited outside.

In the yard she stood, large and menacing, arms folded, blocking their way. Rosie moved to the right, Aggie moved with her. Rosie ducked to the left and back again. Aggie was still there, swollen with fury. Suddenly her hand whipped out and whacked Rosie across the face. Another blow followed. Rosie tottered. Madge ran at Agnes. "You louser!" she screeched. Agnes was unmoved.

"That'll teach you Rose O'Brien. You'd better not make a fool of me again. Next time I'll really bash you up. I'll larrup ya!"

She prodded Rosie's chest vigorously at each word and flounced off, every inch the victor.

A traumatised Rosie followed Madge home for dinner.

Chapter 5

SHE WAS too upset to notice much on the way home. Madge looked at her worriedly. "We'll have to do something about Agnes Balfe. She really hates you. We could ask Jack to bash her up, but I don't think he will, 'cos she's younger than him and he thinks it's sissy to fight girls."

"We'd better do something by Friday anyway," Rosie's voice was gloomy.

"Why Friday?"

Because Friday and the High Swing Challenge will change your life and Aunt Rose's! But she did not say this to Madge. Instead she said, "Oh, it's just that I'd like to get her sorted out this week."

"She'll only stop tormenting you if you fight her and beat her. Drawing that picture was no help."

"No, well I didn't think Miss Hackett would show it to her, never mind to the whole class."

Madge caught the tone of regret.

"I wouldn't feel sorry for her, Rose. Not after all she's done to you. Big brute!"

Rosie felt glad she didn't know all "Aggie the Hag" had done. The nickname seemed a bit mean.

By now they had turned the corner to Gran's house. It

looked at once familiar, yet totally different. A garage with wooden doors took the place of the kitchen. And there was no storm door on the porch. Surrounding the garden was a huge hedge which hadn't been there that morning. The tops of the bay windows were stained-glass to match the front door and all the wooden frames were painted a bright yellow.

Gosh, it's all much nicer than aluminium, Rosie thought.

And Gran was different. When she opened the door Rosie thought for one marvellous moment it was her Mom – that everything was suddenly back to normal. But this wasn't Madge, although she was about the same age. She wore lipstick which Mom never did and her hair was permed. She also wore an apron – Madge hated aprons – and when she turned, there were seams up the back of her legs.

"Howya Ma," said Madge. This was Gran alright. They followed her. The house was so different. There was a tiny kitchen at the end of the hall and no carpet on the floors, just vinyl.

"I hope you're not bringing in muck over my nice clean lino."

Dutifully they wiped their feet. In the dining-room there were no radiators. In Gran's later years the fire was lit only on Sundays and the fireplace was made of ugly blue tiles . . . Now the hearth blazed cheerfully under a beautiful brass canopy and mahogany mantelpiece.

But this is much better! Rosie thought. In one alcove a huge wooden radio sat on a table. The other was empty. She gasped.

"Where's the telly?"

Madge stared at her.

"When are we getting a television?" she amended.

"Don't be barmy Rose, no one around here has a

television," Madge was impatient. "Where do you get your notions?"

At this moment a human whirlwind blew into the room, ducking and weaving, playfully pushing Madge. She squealed, "Stop it Jack."

Jack! Her uncle Jack. He paused for a moment and Rosie giggled. He looked like the picture of William she had seen yesterday afternoon in her aunt's old books. His grey trousers stopped at the knees and he wore a school cap, a sleeveless pullover and a grey shirt. His socks were the same as her own; he must have been about thirteen.

"Why aren't you wearing long trousers?" she asked.

He gave a shout. "Hah! At last my sister recognises my superiority – gives me credit for my superb manly qualities!" He began to duck and weave again. "But our Ma will not purchase long trousers for me until next year. When I go to O'Connell's School, I will have magnificent long trousers. I will have luminous socks, if I can persuade our Ma, and winkle-picker shoes. I will be a massive secondary school boy!"

"Well, you'll have to put on a lot of weight to be massive, you look like a beanpole!"

He cocked an outraged eye at her.

"Beanpole! I am a wonderful specimen of boyhood. And it is 'massive' as in 'terrific' or 'great'!"

"Oh. You mean 'deadly'!"

He was highly indignant.

"Deadly! Am I a rattlesnake? Am I Poison Ivy? I mean 'massive' nit-wit," And he jabbed at her gently.

Rosie pushed him. Immediately he fell onto his back, on the floor, his legs cycling the air.

"Ow! The Massive Rocky Marciano of Whitehall knocked out in Round One by Rose O'Brien, the Deadly Pugilist."

Gran came in from the kitchen.

"Stop your fooling Jack and sit down for your dinner. Your Da'll be in any minute."

An oak table was set for five. The large wooden clock on the mantelpiece struck a single chime and, as though on cue, a tall, smiling, dark haired man entered. Granda! Rosie took a deep breath, her eyes glued to him. He made a mock swipe at Jack and the two circled each other like boxers until suddenly he gripped Jack's pullover and held him at arm's length. Jack couldn't reach him. All he could do was pummel the air. The man laughed and stepped back.

"Hello Twinnies. Hello Madge," and he swung her up in the air.

Then he sat down at the top of the table, Jack opposite. Rosie took her place beside Madge and Gran brought in the dinner. It smelled delicious. Circles of meat with stuffing, peas and potatoes. Rosie ate it all. She had never eaten anything so tasty as the meat. Gran watched her.

"You really love pig's heart, don't you Rose, it's your favourite dinner."

Heart! Pig's heart!

I think I'd rather have fish fingers or a Big Mac," she said faintly.

Jack hooted. "Fish fingers? I'm sure they'd be very tasty, especially the nails and knuckles. And what about fish toes? And other embarrassing parts. What about fish bums?" He choked with laughter. Gran tut-tutted.

"I object strongly Ma," Jack declared when Gran brought in the apple tart, "I object strongly to Madge and Rose getting a full slice each. After all they are not full size themselves. Also they are twins. And twins ought share everything, especially a slice of apple tart. Then I could have the spare one. After all I am a growing boy. Next year I will be in long trousers. Science proves that boys my age need . . . "

"Less of your oul guff Jack," said Granda mildly. Jack was crest-fallen. Rosie giggled. She'd never heard such rubbish.

"And by the way Rose, what's a Big Mac? Is he a character in the *Beano*?" Granda asked.

Rosie stared at them, suddenly horrified. She was living in a house without a television, in a world that had never heard of fish fingers or MacDonalds and with people who ate hearts! How could she survive?

It was better not to think about it too deeply.

Granda lost interest in Big Macs and turned on the radio for the Half-One News. It took a while to heat up and sounded a bit fuzzy.

"It has been confirmed today that the wedding of Grace Kelly and Prince Rainier of Monaco will take place in the tiny principality of Monaco in April. Miss Kelly is from Chicago and has played in Box-Office successes such as *White Christmas* and *High Noon*."

Rosie knew Grace Kelly had been Mom's favourite film star. Now she had a mad urge to tell them that Princess Grace was to die decades later when her car would tumble over a cliff. But Gran seemed genuinely delighted for the actress and she said nothing. Then it struck her: I'll be taking Aunt Rose's place in that accident. Three months in hospital! Or worse, this time it could be fatal. I've got 'til Friday – unless Aunt Rose comes back. Or unless I do something about Agnes Balfe.

Rosie was inclined to dawdle on the way back to school. She was fascinated by the differences in this strange yet familiar world. Smoke was curling from every chimney. There was no boys' secondary school, no houses on Upper Collins Avenue, only fields, and the Ballymun Towers had disappeared. There were so few cars and they were heavy old-fashioned things, most of them black. Some even had steps into them. The roads were full of cyclists on stalwart black bikes. And every man wore a hat or cap, and metal clips around his ankles. There was much less noise. She caught sight of the number 3 bus. It had no remote control doors, just an open area at the back. As it swung around the corner people jumped off before the stop.

School children stood beside a horse and cart, where an old man, his coat tied around the waist with string, exchanged bags of sweets for jam jars. She would have lingered awhile, but Madge was afraid they would be late. Rosie looked quickly at her watch. It was two o'clock. The bell sounded as they went in the school door.

"This afternoon we will start with Singing." Miss Hackett took a tuning fork from her desk. "I will give you the note and we will begin with that wonderful negro spiritual, 'My Old Kentucky Home.'"

Rosie was stunned. She was going to have to bluff her way through this one. The tune was vaguely familiar and she caught the chorus quickly, so quickly, she decided to join in loudly the second time round, instead of just moving her lips. Rosie liked singing.

"Weep no more my lady
Weep no more today
For the sun shines bright
On my old Kentucky home
On my old Kentucky home
Faa-aar Aw aay – aay – hay."

It was a mistake to sing. The class faltered to a halt as Rosie carried the chorus into notes never intended for it.

"Who's out of tune?" Miss Hackett glared in Rosie's general direction, but the girl looked innocent enough.

"Just be careful," she said to no one in particular. "Now

we will do that delightful ditty, 'The Minuet'. Take the
note."

"Lightly Lift your dainty dancing shoe,
Turn a toe,
Simply so,
That is what dear Granma used to do –
Years ago-oho-ho-ho, years ago."

Again Rosie was deceived into thinking she could manage
the chorus second time round and what was meant to be
the most delicate of tunes, sung in the lightest of tones,
galloped madly out of control when she joined in.

"Dear God Almighty! It's one of you O'Brien twins.
Sing that chorus again!" Miss Hackett stood beside their
desk. This time Rosie's voice cracked from nervousness.
Madge's wasn't much better.

"Stop! Both of you. At once! Don't attempt to join in
again. Agnes stand over here beside these clots, so that
they can hear a true sweet voice. Now everyone start
again." And they did, with Aggie slyly jabbing Rosie as she
sang.

"Beautiful. You sing like a bird Agnes."

"Yes but what kind of bird?" whispered Rosie loudly. "A
vulture with asthma!" Aggie gave her a savage dig before
returning to her place.

The Dunce's row was against the wall at the door. Eight
girls sat there meekly, under constant attack from Miss
Hackett for their "stupidity". They were the ones most
often whacked for not knowing spellings; for
mispronouncing words in the Reader or getting their Irish
wrong. Miss Hackett would stand over a girl in the
Dunce's row and ask a question, cane at the ready, almost
daring her to give the wrong answer.

They're afraid to answer, Rosie realised, in case it's not

45

right and if they don't answer she whacks them anyway. What a Bully! She felt furious, as Miss Hackett lashed again at a hapless victim who mumbled a reply.

Suddenly she remembered something and raised her hand.

"Miss Hackett, it's against the law to hit a person in your class. Capital Punishment isn't allowed."

The class gave a collective gasp and Miss Hackett swung around. Her face went a dangerous red. She stormed across the room to Rosie.

"I think you mean Corporal Punishment!" she snarled. "Though in your case perhaps hanging would be more suitable."

Gripping her by the arm she pulled her up and dragged her to the top of the room. The chair had clattered to the floor, followed by all the books on Rosie's desk.

Standing on the platform, Miss Hackett swung her around to face the class. "This girl," she said in a voice filled with fury, "is a liar. She has as good as called me a common criminal. When I slap one of you, I do it for your sake. It is certainly not a crime and it gives me no pleasure. I'm sure you would all agree that a good slap is often needed and makes a better person. Wouldn't you?"

Silence from a terrified class.

"Wouldn't you?"

She waited for an answer.

The class panicked. "Yes Miss. Of course, Miss." She turned to Rosie.

"And you Miss! You could certainly do with a good slapping! Luckily I have the power to administer this punishment. Luckily I believe in 'Spare the Rod and Spoil the Child', because otherwise, Miss Obnoxious O'Brien, you would turn out a proper menace to society. Hold out your hand."

Rosie didn't move, her head was bowed and she

attempted to control her tears. Never in her life before had she been treated like this.

Miss Hackett grabbed her left wrist and brought the cane down on her hand with all her force. Rosie tried to pull back, but couldn't. Six times the relentless cane cut into her palm. Miss Hackett was heaving with exertion. Rosie was crying helplessly, her hand limp and numb at her side. But the ordeal was not over. Miss Hackett grabbed the other hand and as the stick came down she shouted triumphantly, "That will teach you Madam, to question my authority!" Then she pushed the weeping girl away from her.

"If you have any complaints Rose O'Brien, I suggest you take them to the police!" Rosie could utter no protest. She was choking with tears of pain and anger and humiliation. Madge had picked up her books and settled her chair. She managed to whisper, "Don't you mind her Rose. She's a cruel Brute!"

"It'll be against the law one day," Rosie sobbed rocking back and forth, hands under her armpits, crying and snuffling. A girl behind patted her on the back quickly. Others sneaked sympathetic looks at her, trying to show they were on her side. Only Agnes Balfe looked triumphant.

The rest of the afternoon passed peacefully enough. Miss Hackett had vented her rage, which had started that morning as a seed of aggravation when Rose O'Brien had dawdled, as she thought, in the toilet. The girl was getting far too insolent. From now on she would keep a close eye on her, starting with the Sums test next morning.

At four o'clock, the school day ended. Dejected, the "twins" left.

"Serves you right Miss Know-All," Agnes Balfe jeered and pushed against Rosie. But the two girls were surrounded by well wishers. Aggie was told to scram.

"Should I tell Gran, er Ma, what happened?" Rosie asked as they neared home.

"I wouldn't. You know she always takes the teacher's part. She wouldn't believe Miss Hackett is so horrible. You'll only get into more trouble. You better wash your face when you get in, it's all streaked."

After homework and tea and listening to *Dan Dare* on the radio, Rosie asked if she could go to bed early, she had a bit of a headache.

She shut the bedroom door. There were neat twin beds, an old fashioned dressing-table, a wardrobe and oak shelves full of the twins' books. Beside each bed was a chest of drawers. Rummaging in the one nearest the window, Rosie found Aunt Rose's diary, the lettering bright gold, the clasp shiny, the pages crisp and white. It was filled in exactly as it had been when Rosie found it – but only for a week, to Sunday the 8th January. She had a notion she should fill in Monday the 9th, but decided it would do later.

Curious about the twins' belongings, Rosie looked in the wardrobe.

"Gross!" she said, noting the frumpy tweed skirts. "Not one pair of jeans or leggings." She lifted the scratchy hand knitted socks from the shelf. "Desperate," she groaned. The knickers beside them were huge, long and thick. "You'd fit at least three people into a pair! And they must be bullet proof." She saw the Christmas suits at the back of the wardrobe and sighed. "Boring. All their clothes are dark and heavy. They must've lasted forever."

Getting ready for bed she thought about the problems ahead. Why does Agnes Balfe hate Rose when all the other girls like her? If I could find out I might be able to change her mind. Then she wouldn't try to harm Rose. Maybe I could even make friends with her.

But somehow Rosie doubted it. There was so much

anger in Agnes, so much determination to hurt her aunt. Why?

I wonder if Rose kept a diary for 1955? As soon as she thought of it she began searching through the drawers. She found some bits and pieces – copies, a box of beads, a polish tin filled with clay, but no diary. Disappointed, Rosie flicked idly through the copies: Sums, Irish, English. Suddenly she caught her breath.

There on the first page of the last copy were the carefully formed words:

Agnes Balfe

or

The Meanist Persin On Earth

By

Rose O'Brien

She began to read:

I am getting a diary for Christmas so I can write all the horribil things Agnes Balfe does. She is brutal. When she came in September I tried to make frends with her the first day. I knew she had been eggspelled from Corpuss Christy school. The Reillys' cousins go there an' they told Eustiss what happened an' he told me.

Somebody dared her to eat in class an' said she was chickin' if she didn't. So she braught in eight cream slices an' ate them during spellin'. She put up the lid of her desk to hide behind but she took too long. The teacher got suspishus an' asked her a spellin'. Agneses mouth was stuffed an she couldn't anwser so she got eggspelled instead. I thought that wasn't fare 'cos she was only eatin' an neither can you eggspell people for not spellin'. Thank God.

Anyway I told her she was great to manidge eight cream slices an' next of all she tried to twist my arm. How was I suppost to know it was all a big secret? She said if I told any persin about those cream slices an' speshly about her robbin' money to buy them she would break my bloody face. I ask you!

The nerve of her. How could I think of tellin' anyone when I didn't know. So I gave her a look an' walked off real dignyfied. Then I heard a roar an she just thundered at me an' knocked me over in a heap.

Ever since then she has tried to rune my life. Scribbelin' all over my work an stealing my pencils. An' she is raging 'cos everyone takes my side except Miss Hackett who thinks I am the trouble-maker.

I would love to wallip Agnes Balfe. She is a terrible afflickshun.

The end

Now she understood. Agnes Balfe had been expelled for stealing and hated Rose for knowing about it. The girl was a thief and a bully and Rosie was furious at the way she'd treated her aunt. Even if it were possible she didn't want to make friends with her now.

There was such a lot to think about. Settling into bed she tried to concentrate, but the events of the day had been too tiring and she fell asleep almost immediately.

Chapter 6

"I DON'T SUPPOSE there's any Frosties," Rosie said half-heartedly as Granda ladled out the porridge for breakfast.

"Frosty what?" Granda leaned over her.

"Oh nothing."

No Frosties. Probably no Chocolate Flavoured Shreddies or Coco Pops. No Muesli, Crunchy Nut Cornflakes or Golden Oatmeal Crisp.

Before going to school Rosie had to line up with Jack and Madge for a dose of cod-liver oil. Yuck! She swallowed rapidly to keep herself from vomiting. Fish slick coated her teeth.

"Why are you making such awful faces Rose? You usually like cod-liver oil." Gran was cross.

Rosie began to wonder about the wisdom of rescuing Aunt Rose. Maybe it wasn't such a good idea to bring into her life someone who loved hearts for dinner and could be enthusiastic about cod-liver oil. Especially if she was as bossy as Mom.

Jack looked even more like William in his belted overcoat and school cap. They parted with him at the corner.

"Eustace, wait for me!" he shouted. Rosie watched the two boys standing together. They took marbles from their pockets and began to play along the gutter on their way to the boys' Primary School.

This time Rosie noticed the hordes of children. They streamed out of houses in threes and fours. And the twins were very popular. A lot of girls from the class caught up with them to chat.

"You were very brave yesterday Rose, to stand up to Miss Hackett," said a dark-eyed girl, her mischievous face lighting up. "I thought she was going to have a fit when you said it was against the law to slap anyone."

"Rose was barmy to say that Linda Reilly, she was bound to get into trouble." Madge was remembering the awful punishment.

"She was the only one to stand up to Miss Hackett. That woman is an awful brute. She must have been trained by Hitler."

Rosie was very proud of herself. She felt a surge of friendliness towards Linda – obviously a superior person who could recognise a heroine when she saw one. All the same it'd be better to avoid trouble with Miss Hackett today.

Although warmly dressed, Rosie shivered suddenly. They were passing the playground and a chill wind whistled, rocking the seesaws. One of the swings creaked forward, then suddenly swung high into the empty air. Rosie's mouth opened.

"Did you see that?" Madge whispered.

"A ghost from the past," Linda said jokingly, then frowned at Rosie's expression. "Why are you so scared? You don't believe me surely! It's only the wind."

Rosie stared transfixed as withered leaves suddenly rustled in corners and blew across the concrete to swirl around her. The playground was cold and menacing in the grey morning light and her heart froze.

"Come on," Linda tugged at her, "You're not afraid of

Miss Hackett, so an old wind can't frighten you!"

If only you knew, Rosie thought as she hurried on. Miss Hackett isn't half as dangerous as that playground.

After prayers came Irish. Miss Hackett left Rosie alone, though every now and then her eyes would rest on her and glitter with ill-feeling. She was biding her time. Just now she gave all her attention to the unfortunates in the Dunce's row who were struggling with Irish writing.

"You are not to write with your left hand," she told one girl, bringing her cane down hard. "How many times do I have to tell you? You must learn to use your right hand. Otherwise you will remain stupid all your life. If God had intended us to be left-handed, we would all be like you."

So gross! Rosie thought. I suppose if we were meant to go to the moon we'd be rockets. Not that Miss Hackett could tell an astronaut from an elbow. She is so *stupid*!

This realisation was a thunderbolt to Rosie who had previously thought, if she'd ever considered the matter at all, that teachers must be very intelligent. After all her Mom and Stormin' Norman were reasonably bright, if a bit eccentric.

The next hour passed easily enough. A Miss Booth arrived to give elocution lessons. After collecting a penny from everyone in the class she made them recite a poem called 'Lepanto'. She had a very posh accent and didn't like theirs.

"Diction girls. Diction! Think of the BBC Home programme. That is the accent to cultivate. Remember, 'Poor diction causes friction.' Now let us try again."

And fifty-six young voices determinedly exaggerated their Dublin accents. They roared out with enthusiasm:

"Dim drums trobbing in deh hills half heyrd
Were only on a nameliss troan a crowanliss prince
has sturred."

53

Rosie couldn't make head nor tail of it and Miss Booth looked about to cry.

"Trobbing!" she moaned, "Crowanliss! Oh what's the use?" She gave up for another week.

"Now for your Sums test." Miss Hackett was back on the platform under the board. "I will put up five shop bills and remember!" Here she narrowed her eyes at Rosie, "Whoever fails must wear the Donkey's Tail." Rosie studied the first four lines. She gave up. It was a foreign language.

    2 Doz eggs @ 2d each
    1 cwt coal @ 19s/11d a stone
    3 st potatoes @ 1s/2d a lb
    2 gross apples @ 1d each

Miss Hackett collected the copies and smiled at Rosie's blank pages. She almost hugged herself with delight, but said nothing. "Now girls, while I'm correcting these I want you to take out your catechisms and learn all of pages 36 and 37."

Rosie opened the book on religion.

Q. How should we treat our enemies?
A. Be good to those who hate us and pray for those who persecute and calumniate us.

Boring. And not much help in dealing with Miss Hackett. She took up her pen – a wooden thing with a funny nib at the end – and dipped it in the inkwell. Her first attempt to write left a large blot on page 36. She shook off some ink and tried again on the blank page at the back of the catechism. It was a bit scratchy but worked well enough.

She glanced at Miss Hackett. The teacher was lost in her corrections. Fifty-five girls mouthing the catechism to themselves in silence. Not out of interest, but out of terror. Rosie turned to an empty page at the back of her book and began to write:

Miss Hackett

Miss Hackett makes our life a pain
I think she really is insane
With her awful temper and dreadful Sums
And the way she tries to whack our thumbs.
(I know you think when I mention "Sums,"
I want to rhyme the word with "Bums"
But I could never be so crude,
To use a word so awful rude!)
She swings her cane around the room
And owns a bike instead of a broom
Someday I know she'll go quite mad
She'll wallop and whack and be so bad!
She'll swirl around in a dance fantastic,
Until there's a sudden snap of elastic
Her face'll be purple, she'll hear our snickers
'Cos she'll have dropped her flamin' knickers!

Rosie put her pen down. Miss Hackett was still at the Sums test. Cautiously, she pushed her catechism over to Madge, who stared in disbelief, first at the poem and then at Rosie. Suddenly she began to giggle helplessly.

"Let's see," whispered the girl behind. Rosie tore out the page quietly and sneaked it back. As the poem went down the row, more girls began to titter. Others grew restless wondering what the joke was. Miss Hackett looked up and Rosie paled. If she was whacked yesterday over slapping, she'd be burned at the stake for this! Or worse.

Miss Hackett descended on them.

"What's happening here! Why are you all smirking and laughing?"

"They're looking at a piece of paper Miss. Linda has it." Aggie the Hag excitedly told on them.

"Not another drawing! Rose O'Brien?"

"No Miss, I didn't draw anything."

"It's words Miss," said Aggie.

"Linda have you got this piece of paper?"

"No Miss."

"What words are on it then?"

"I didn't see any words Miss."

"Whoever has this piece of paper stand up at once!"

No one stood up. The paper had vanished.

"Maybe Agnes is dreaming Miss," said Linda.

"Then what are you laughing at?"

There was silence. Rosie prayed. Then Linda said, "It's Aggie Miss. Her hair's funny." It was feeble, but it saved Rosie.

The gong went for dinnertime and although Miss Hackett looked doubtful she let them off home. Out in the yard Linda handed back Rosie's sheet.

"When I saw her coming down I grabbed it from Mary and stuffed it in her schoolbag, mine wasn't open. It's a great laugh Rose I just read it, but she would've murdered you."

Rosie was extremely grateful. It had been a narrow escape.

Dinner was a tasty stew. If there was anything funny in it Rosie didn't want to know. Granda asked her some spellings and was very pleased when she got them all right.

"Amazing improvement, Rose. Keep it up!"

Jack was humming a song to himself.

"Where's Rocky Marciano Two gone?" Granda asked.

"I'm finished with boxing. Instead I will become famous as a singer. People will pay money to see me." He warbled:

"I'm gonna rock around the clock to-night,
I'm gonna rock rock rock in the pale moon light
I'm gonna rock around the clock to-ni-i-ight."

"That song is ancient," Rosie told him.

"You Rose, are a ninny. That song is the latest and I will one day be the new Bill Haley."

"No you won't. You'll be an engineer and you'll get married and have three children. Anyway you have a terrible voice."

"You have no taste Rose. You do not recognise quality even when it shatters your eardrum. And I will never get married. Girls are no fun." He went back to his humming.

Rosie looked at her watch. One forty. Time to get back to school. Then swiftly she turned her back on Jack. Her watch! Her digital quartz calculator watch! She was wearing it! How many times had she looked at it without realising its significance. It certainly did not belong to 1956. Not if hardly anyone owned a TV. Well at least she wasn't crazy. She did belong to the future and perhaps the watch was a sign that she would get back there.

In school, Miss Hackett was impatient to get them all seated.

"I have your Sums tests corrected. I am pleased to say every one of you passed, except Rose O'Brien, who did not attempt one single sum. To my mind this is sheer boldness. Rose O'Brien has a reputation for being excellent at Sums. She has always got high marks in every test. She cannot spell very well, but she has always been top of the class at Sums." She paused and then said menacingly, "Or perhaps she copied her tests every other time!"

"I never copied in my life," Rosie blurted, "And I can spell perfectly!"

"Don't be impertinent. You cannot spell. Why only the other week you spelled 'example', e-g-g-s-a-m-p-e-l. I have it on record, so don't contradict me."

"Can so spell!"

"Then spell 'hallucinating', because that's what you're doing."

"H-a-l-l-u-c-i-n-a-t-i-n-g." Rosie clearly enunciated every letter.

"A fluke! And don't you dare contradict me by spelling properly. You will stay back at four o'clock and write a composition as a punishment. Now come up here 'til I pin this Donkey's Tail on you."

Wearily Rosie went up to the platform where Miss Hackett pinned a long piece of rope to the belt at the back of her uniform. Above it she fastened a notice "Donkey's Tail". Rosie had to wear it all afternoon as a badge of dishonour, even at toilet break. Miss Hackett made a point in the corridor of explaining it loudly to another teacher.

"She came last in the Sums test. Not one sum attempted. And she thinks she's wonderful. But she can't spell and she can't do simple shop bills. She's a stupid dunce, really."

If Rosie had not been so outraged, she might have wept. How could this woman be a teacher? Teachers were supposed to be helpful! She seethed with anger.

"Never again," she vowed, "will I complain about Stormin' Norman."

Chapter 7

"Now Rose O'Brien, you will stay until half past four. You will write a composition on 'Why I am a dunce.' I will be back to collect it." Miss Hackett slammed the door. Rosie was alone in the bleak classroom. The yellow light bulb contrasted with the gathering darkness outside the windows. Rosie could just make out the smoke, curling from distant chimneys.

She wrote swiftly, giving Miss Hackett the kind of essay she wanted. "I am a dunce because I don't study, pay attention, do proper homework . . ." Blah blah blah. Well, she could hardly write, "I am not a dunce. I come from the future where the old money has gone the same way as the Dodo and anyway it would be hard for anyone to be clever with you teaching them." No, that would not do at all. She made quite a few deliberate spelling mistakes just to keep Miss Hackett happy. There was no point in making her suspicious.

She was just finished at a quarter past. Staring out the window she thought of Aunt Rose. She had absolutely no idea how to get them both out of this mess. She looked into the darkness for a glimmer of light. In her head she heard the same young voice she'd heard in her bedroom, the whisper she heard in the tunnel.

"Rosie you are helping, you're changing the past."

That was true! Aunt Rose had not failed a Sums test. Nor did she have to wear a Donkey's Tail.

"You must write in the diary," the voice said.

Lost in thought, Rosie nearly jumped out of her skin when another, quite different voice sneered, "Kept back for being stupid. Serves you right. You think too much of yourself for such a horrible little trollop."

It was Agnes Balfe. She must have sneaked back in. Now she stood at Miss Hackett's desk and opened a drawer.

"Know what I've got here? The Black Baby Box and all the money collected on Monday for the poor children of Africa." She was busy widening the slit with a ruler. Then she emptied out the large brown coins. A black child grinned upside-down at Rosie. Agnes put the coins in her pocket and replaced the box.

"Well Miss Smart-Alec, guess who's going to get the blame for this!" She laughed and ran out of the room.

Miss Hackett returned five minutes later. Rosie handed up her essay in silence and left. Miss Hackett decided to put the copy in her drawer until the next day. As she pushed back the Black Baby Box it seemed strangely empty. She lifted it. Not a penny inside! Miss Hackett caught her breath! Rose O'Brien was the only person who could have stolen the money. The only one who had been alone in the class for any length of time. She flushed with anger. The nerve of the girl! A common thief. This was a matter for the head nun! For expulsion! Maybe even for the police! She smiled grimly.

At home Gran couldn't understand why Rosie had done so badly in her test. "But you're great at Sums. What happened Rose?"

Rosie shrugged, "I just didn't know how to do them."

Gran thought. "I suppose you had some sort of blank," she said finally. "It can happen to anyone."

Rosie had more pressing problems to think about. What was she going to do about the missing money? There wasn't the slightest doubt but she would be blamed.

She told Madge what happened. They were in the bedroom changing out of their uniforms. Looking at the dumpy tweed skirt she was about to put on, Rosie suddenly felt fed up.

"Why don't we have proper clothes?" She turned to Madge, "Why don't we have jeans, or sweatshirts, or track suits, or leggings or joggers instead of this horrible old gear?"

Madge thought she had gone mad.

"What are you talking about Rose? We're not in America. Girls don't wear jeans. Only workmen. And what's a sweatshirt? It sounds very smelly altogether. Where did you get all these names? You should worry more about Miss Hackett. She really hates you."

And that was when Rosie told her about Agnes Balfe and the Black Baby Box. Madge slowly sat down on the bed, her eyes wide with horror.

"You'll be expelled. We've got to do something . . . We'd better tell Jack. The three of us should be able to think of a plan."

Madge went down to get Jack and Rosie took out the diary. She could not believe her eyes. The page for yesterday was filled in. Exactly the same as when she'd first read it! How awful! Then she remembered her Aunt's words: "You must write in the diary." She had to record what happened today. She must change the past in the diary.

She had just finished when Madge and Jack came into the room.

"I heard what happened Rose," Jack was sympathetic. "But do not worry. The Dan Dare of Whitehall will not be defeated by an ignoramus like Agnes Balfe!"

61

"Do you know her?" Rosie asked.

"I know her to see, and I know her brother, Mel. He is famous for his pong. 'Smelly Melly' we call him, or 'Big Mouth Balfe.' He tells on everyone."

Jack hadn't any idea what to do, but promised to help anyway. He was deep in thought at teatime. Granda came in and heard about the Sums test.

"Poor Rose. Anyone can have a bad day you know. It's a pity you had to stay back when you usually do so well. Still, it's probably for your own good."

He sat down to read the Evening Press which was still full of Grace Kelly.

"Monaco Wedding for Grace," was the headline and there were pictures of the actress as a baby and a small girl.

What would have happened if she'd known her future? Would she have done anything different? Rosie wondered. She shivered. Her own future could change dramatically on Friday. She looked at Gran and Granda, chatting now and then about the news, very contented. Neither of them had a notion of what lay ahead.

Jack was trying to signal to her across the table. When she caught his eye, he smiled and made a thumbs up sign. He had a plan. Rosie tried to be grateful, but really, it was bad enough trying to cope with Friday, without having to worry about trouble from Miss Hackett. The only thing about this robbery was that it hadn't happened to her aunt. Somehow, after Rose's accident, a different person had emerged, who'd wanted nothing more to do with her twin. It was as if her personality had been split in two and one of those personalities had been left behind. It was up to Rosie to join them together again. The more she could change things that happened to Aunt Rose, the better chance she had of changing the past – and therefore the future.

She followed Jack and Madge upstairs.

"Naturally," said Jack, "I have come up with a Master Plan. My first idea was to bash up this Agnes Balfe. But then she might not be able to limp into school tomorrow to put back the money."

Rosie looked at Jack the Beanpole. All Aggie had to do was use her "Super Strategy" on him. He'd just keel over. He'd be the one limping.

"Anyway Da'd kill me if I hit a girl. So I thought and I thought and I thought and . . . "

"It was obviously a terrible strain," Madge said and stifled a yawn.

Jack ignored the sarcasm and finished triumphantly, "Then I suddenly remembered. Last Sunday we went into Morgan's to buy Nancy Balls."

"Rivetting!" Madge was withering. "Your mind is amazing. We ask you to help us with a terrible problem, a major crisis in Rose's life, and you can only think of Nancy Balls. If you had one brain cell Jack, you'd be lop-sided."

In spite of her problems Rosie giggled.

Jack sighed, "Stop interrupting. When we were going into the shop Aggie was running up the hill as if she couldn't get away fast enough. She beat Roger Bannister's four-minute mile."

"Yes yes yes. So she can run. So what, Jack! It's Rose who'll have to run tomorrow – away from the Bamboo-Basher!"

"The point is, if you will just listen Madge – and you should listen to your brother Jack because he always has something wise and wonderful to say . . . " He paused maddeningly, then noticed Madge's murderous look and continued hastily, "Anyway, when we went into the shop, Mrs Morgan if you remember, said she'd just been robbed. Someone had come in while she was in the back room. She heard the bell, but by the time she came out the person had gone and so had six packets of Gold Flake, six

Dairy Milk, four Crunchies and two Cough-no-more bars. I think Agnes Balfe robbed them."

They were silent then, deep in thought. Then Madge said, "I think you're right, Jack. I didn't make any connection at the time. But how can this help Rose?"

"Simple. We go around to her house. Tell her we saw her through Morgan's window. And if she doesn't put the money back before Miss Hackett gets in, we'll tell the police. Blackmail is the only way."

"Brilliant!" Rosie declared.

Even Madge was impressed. "I'm sorry I said you didn't have a brain cell," she smiled, "it's a good idea."

"Naturally. I think I will become a blackmailer when I leave school. I have a great talent for it."

The next task was to get out of the house. Gran didn't like any of them out after tea in case they got a cold or 'flu from the damp night air. This time Madge had the idea.

"We'll tell Ma that Rose has a message for Agnes Balfe from Miss Hackett. It's sort of the truth. And you didn't give it to her earlier because you were already late home from school."

"Brilliant!" Rosie declared again.

Gran and Granda were listening to Wilfred Pickles on the radio and didn't want to be disturbed.

"We have to give Agnes Balfe a message from school," Rosie told them.

"What message? Never mind. Hurry up. Be back as fast as you can."

They set off through the dark streets, Rosie one step behind in case the others figured she didn't know the way. Agnes Balfe lived at the bottom of a cul-de-sac. Though the garden was small, it was overgrown and the street light cast eerie shadows on the bushes and trees. Rosie was afraid but Madge knocked loudly on the front door. An unshaven hulk of a man jerked it open.

"Are you lot trying to bring back the ghost of Christmas past?" he roared.

The words chilled Rosie to the bone. She remembered Linda's words outside the playground. She'd had the same awful feeling then. She was the ghost! Not from the past but from the future.

"Well, what's all the noise for? What's up?"

"We've come to see Agnes. We've got a message from Miss Hackett for her."

"Well no need to knock the house down. It can't be that urgent. Wait here. I'll get her." He went off grumbling.

Agnes arrived at the door.

"Oh look who's here: the Heavy Gang. What do you want?"

"We want you to put back the money you stole from the Black Baby Box." Madge said.

"Fat chance. It's about time your precious sister got into serious trouble. She won't be so popular when everyone thinks she's a robber!"

"You're the robber," Madge said furiously.

"And you're making quite a habit of it," added Jack. "We saw you on Sunday in Morgan's."

"So what! You can't prove anything."

"No," said Jack, "but we'll tell the police anyway." He raised his voice and said calmly and distinctly. "And since you stole six packets of Gold Flake, you've hardly smoked them all yet. I'd say you've got them hidden somewhere. Maybe under your bed?" Suddenly he roared, "Give us one of the cigarettes you stole!"

Inside, a door opened and a man yelled, "Agnes, Get rid of those Bowsies or I'll do it for you!"

"Maybe I wasn't loud enough," Jack said and he opened his mouth very wide . . .

"Ssshhh. Keep your voice down!" Aggie was clearly

panicking. "Da'll kill me. Don't tell the police. I'll put the money back."

"You'd better. We may not have much proof, but we're witnesses and the police won't ignore three of us."

The large girl was convinced. Jack's calm certainty made her afraid.

"Alright, alright, just go. I said I'll put the money back." She was bitterly disappointed. All immediate prospects of revenge were fading. But as the three figures walked jauntily down the garden path, she muttered, "I'll get you Rose O'Brien. Somehow I'll get you!"

Chapter 8

ON HER way to school next morning Rosie said little. She was in deep thought, wondering if Agnes Balfe would get the money back in time. She jumped a foot into the air when Madge suddenly bawled:

"Mrs O'Kelly broke her belly
Sliding on a lump of jelly
Mrs O'Kelly's very smelly
Smelly like a smelly wellieee!"

The only possible Mrs O'Kelly was a middle aged woman striding ahead of them. Madge obviously thought the woman was deaf because she bellowed the last two lines again:

"Mrs O Kelly's very smelly
Smelly like a smelly wellieee!"

Up to half a mile in front of them everyone turned a head, even a man on a bicycle. Madge grabbed Rosie's arm and rushed her around the corner. Rosie was dumbfounded. After all, this was her mother. The same mother who was always giving out to her for getting into trouble. Now she was yelling insults like a lunatic after a respectable woman.

Luckily Mrs O'Kelly just tossed her head and marched on. Hopefully she didn't know who they were. Madge was beside herself with glee. "That shook her, the oul meany."

"Why did you do it ?" asked Rosie.

"You know why. Because she took all my toffees that day she was supervising us. Said it was against school rules to eat in class."

"Stormin' Norman does that all the time if you eat in class," Rosie said without thinking.

"Who's Stormin' Norman? Where'd you read about him? And anyway I wasn't eating was I? I hadn't even one ready to pop into my mouth. Those toffees were in my schoolbag if you remember. And when she asked if anyone had sweets in school, you said I had, and would she like one!" Madge sniffed sourly, highly aggrieved at the memory. But Rosie had lost interest. There was, after all, the more pressing matter of the Black Baby Box.

Miss Hackett was already installed on her platform when they got in. Agnes Balfe was in her place, looking blankly ahead, giving no clue. Miss Hackett seemed to be jigging around, foostering with papers on her desk, glancing at Rosie, unable to stand still. When everyone was seated she waited for total silence. The last chair stopped scraping. She had their full attention. Still she waited, staring coldly. A wave of tension swept over the class. What was wrong now? Which of them was in trouble? No pin dropped as each one of them – except Rosie, Madge and Agnes Balfe – searched her mind for some wrongdoing.

"A most terrible thing has happened girls." At last Miss Hackett began. "There has been a robbery." Her eyes swivelled around the class and rested briefly on Rosie. "Someone in this class has robbed all the money in the Black Baby Box and I know who it is!"

There was a sharp intake of breath.

Rosie gazed steadily at Miss Hackett.

"You know how much the Black Babies in Africa depend upon our help and you have given your pennies generously every Monday of every week. Now this money – your money – has been robbed, depriving those children of your help. And who has committed this despicable crime?" She paused for effect, then pointed dramatically. "The culprit is Rose O'Brien!"

A current of shock ran through the class. No one believed it , but that didn't count. What did count was what Miss Hackett would do to Rose O'Brien.

"Something as serious as this is a matter for our head nun, Mother Culpertino. In fact, I have already notified her and she will be here any moment. It is also, if I am not mistaken, a matter for expulsion. Indeed the police may have to be called in."

Rosie stared unwaveringly at Miss Hackett. She would not lower her eyes, knowing it would be taken as a sign of guilt. Miss Hackett breathed heavily and her face became a mottled, dull red.

"You are an insolent pup Rose O'Brien. Stand up at once!"

At that moment the head nun glided in. Rosie had only seen her in the distance on the corridors. Up close, she was amazed at all the clothes she wore. Covered from head to toe in heavy black. A bit like Darth Vadar, Rosie thought. The nun nodded to Miss Hackett, who used the moment for further drama.

"Rose O'Brien," she began. "Tell Mother Culpertino who was alone in the class at four o'clock yesterday!"

"I was, Mother."

"For how long were you kept back?" Miss Hackett continued the interrogation.

"Half an hour."

"Ample time to rob the money in the Black Baby Box.

You're the only one who had the opportunity."

"I didn't take any money," Rosie said steadily, this time looking at Mother Culpertino.

The nun considered her thoughtfully and said nothing. Miss Hackett was seething.

"Of course you took it! You are a trouble-maker and a liar. Look at this, Mother!" Triumphantly she pulled out the drawer and lifted the Black Baby Box. It was heavy with pennies. Miss Hackett paled. She placed the box on her desk and backed away from it as though it had some evil life of its own. "I don't understand . . . You must have put the money back . . . Yes Yes . . . That's what you did. You put it back this morning."

"She couldn't have, Miss." It was Linda. "She was in after you this morning."

Miss Hackett stared, her lips moving soundlessly. Mother Culpertino took control.

"Obviously there's been some misunderstanding. The money isn't missing and Rose didn't take it. Miss Hackett I'd like to see you at half past twelve in my office. Now you may all go on with your lessons." She smiled kindly at Rosie and left.

For a long while afterwards Miss Hackett was incapable of speech. She set them work to do and sat down dazed, staring into space. Now and then she studied Rosie, a puzzled expression on her face. Rosie wanted no more trouble. In spite of her calm appearance, she had been terrified. What if Agnes Balfe had not put the money back?

Notes began to arrive on her desk by a silent chain of communication.

"Serves her right. Good on ya."

"Don't know how you did it. Massive!"

"Terrific, Rose!"

They all thought she had taken the money and

somehow put it back, to make Miss Hackett look a fool. Only one note was different to the rest.

I'm not finished yet. I dare you to take the High Swing Challenge but you're probably too chicken.
                                        Agnes Balfe

Rosie was deeply afraid. It seemed as if nothing could change Fate. Events were leading to the same end, unstoppable. What if she took up the challenge? Who would be injured? Herself or her aunt? If she, Rosie McGrath, fell from the High Swing and ended up in a coma, she could be stuck in the past. She did not want to grow up in the fifties and sixties. And what of Aunt Rose? What would happen to her? She could answer none of these questions.

She would not take up the challenge. No way. On the back of Agnes's note she wrote:

This challenge is silly. I refuse it. I'll fight you instead at the back of the school at four o'clock – but then you are probably too chicken.
                                        Rose O'Brien

The note made its way back. Agnes read it and looked sneeringly at her. She made a throat-cutting gesture and smiled triumphantly. This was far better than the challenge. This meant she could pulverise Rose O'Brien. Revenge at last.

Miss Hackett had them writing the whole morning. In the afternoon there was Dancing class in the hall. They were divided into couples to perform the minuet, singing the words while the music was played on an old gramophone. The "male" partner bowed exaggeratedly and for some reason waved a hanky in the air. The "lady" curtsied before the first steps were taken. Rosie might have found it all very entertaining had she not been lost in thought about the fight.

The news had spread like wildfire round the class. No one considered she had a chance. They thought she was brave but suicidal. Agnes Balfe would batter her. She would limp home in tatters – if she was lucky. Everyone wanted to witness the drama. All afternoon there was an atmosphere of high tension which found no outlet in the sedate ritual of the courtly minuet. Girls were tripping over one another with excitement, whispering to each other, unable to concentrate. The time was unbearably long.

Madge thought Rosie was mad. "Only a pure lunatic would challenge Agnes Balfe. She'll mangle you. Why did you do it?"

"Because I didn't want to accept the High Swing Challenge."

"You're daft, Rose. It'd be cinchy compared to this."

Oh no it wouldn't, Rosie thought. "I might win you know!"

Madge looked at her scornfully, "You have as much hope of beating her as Ireland has of beating America in a war."

Rosie felt a bit miffed at this lack of faith.

"All she has to do," Madge added somewhat wearily, "is to sit on you and you'll be squashed to death."

But Rosie remembered what her Dad had once told her about Mohammed Ali who, he said, had been the greatest boxer in the world. "And you know why? Because he never let his opponent get near him. He moved real fast around the ring, tiring out the other guy. He'd duck and weave, and weave and jab and the other fellow could never catch him. 'Dance like a butterfly, sting like a bee.' That was his motto!" Rosie spent a lot of time that afternoon thinking about Mohammed Ali.

At last the four o'clock bell sounded. She gathered up her bag and coat and made her way with Madge to the back of the school. Agnes Balfe strode ahead, the rest of the class respectfully behind the fighters. Waves of their excitement reached Rosie:

"Agnes Balfe'll batter her."

"That one hates Rose. She'll murder her."

"Poor Rose'll need an ambulance."

They crossed the road and climbed over the low wall onto a patch of wasteland. It was unlikely they would be seen from the school. Most of the teachers would have left by the front gate. The nearest house was some distance away. Nevertheless a look out was posted on the wall.

The class made a circle and dropped their bags on the ground. Rosie and Agnes Balfe set down their belongings under the tree and stood facing each other in the centre of the ring. Agnes wiped her nose on the back of her hand. She pushed her sleeves up to her elbows. Rosie was about to do the same when Agnes charged, bowling her over onto her back. The momentum carried the bigger girl to the edge of the circle.

Although she was winded, Rosie had time to get herself to her feet. She doubled up, pretending to be worse than she was, all the time keeping an eye on Agnes. Again she charged. This time Rosie stepped neatly aside and caught Aggie a stinging blow on the back of the neck. The big girl turned, deciding to tackle, but could not reach her.

Rosie ducked and weaved, dancing, jabbing, poking. The girls roared in delight. Once she caught her enemy in the eye with a thumb. The class bully howled, momentarily blinded. Rosie cracked her across the cheek and kicked her shin. Suddenly, Agnes caught her with a whack to the side of the head and Rosie almost fell. She managed to move back and shook her head clear. For the next five minutes she kept away from Agnes, ducking and skipping.

Agnes was bewildered. She had never seen anyone fight like this before. She lumbered and charged, stumbled and flailed. It was like a battle between an elephant and a buzzing insect. The insect was very squashable, if only it would stay still. Aggie was tiring. She was not used to long drawn out fights. Her face was red and sweaty with exertion.

"Come on Rose!"

"Don't let her touch you Rose!"

"Bravo Rose!"

The crowd cheered her on. So many of them had expected a one-sided, one minute battle. But this would teach Aggie Balfe a lesson. For too long she had terrorised by bullying.

"You're winning Rose."

This last infuriated Aggie. She stood still, watching. Rosie's jigging movements began to look silly. The crowd shifted uneasily.

"Come on Rose, give her another jab."

No way. That's what she's waiting for, thought Rosie. Instead she backed slowly to the tree where the ring of girls started and ended.

"Move the stuff Madge, get the tree clear." Her instructions were low and urgent. Madge casually inched their bags and coats away with her foot. Rosie stood still in front of the tree.

Agnes Balfe advanced towards her, then stopped. Rosie knew she must draw her on. She made a sudden rush and jabbed at Aggie.

"What are you waiting for?" she jibed. "Too slow to move?" She darted back to the tree, every nerve of her body ready.

"You little runt. You disgusting insect!" Aggie ranted.

She was very near to Rosie now and victory was sure. The class was on either side of the miserable horror. There was a tree behind her. Rose O'Brien could not escape her Super Strategy. Of this Aggie was certain.

The large girl bellowed and charged. Her plaits stuck out on either side of her head. Her boots thundered across the short stretch of waste ground. Fists clenched, she was ready to destroy.

Rosie waited till the very last moment; till she could feel Aggie's breath on her face and the swish of her skirt.

Then she stepped aside in the space Madge had made for her. Agnes ran straight into the tree. The girl reeled back. Her face was scraped from the bark, her nose pumped blood. Her head was throbbing from the impact. All fight left her. There was a brief cheer, but Rosie rushed over to the enemy.

"Are you alright?"

Agnes just looked at her.

"Agnes, we don't have to hate each other. We could try to be friends if you like."

The other girl nearly spat at her. "Friends! Drop dead. You'll be sorry you tried any of your sneaky tricks on me. You didn't fight fair and you're nothing but a rotten flamin' coward."

"You don't fight fair yourself Aggie. You and your Super Strategy. You're a mega-bully and a rotten loser."

"I haven't lost yet. Just you wait! Lousy bowsy! Pig! I'll get you."

But Rosie was already out of earshot, making her way home basking in the admiration of her classmates.

Chapter 9

"MY GOODNESS, Agnes Balfe, what happened to you?"

Agnes could not bear to follow the others, all chattering like ninnies about her defeat. She decided to go back through the school yard and out the front gate. That way she could be alone with her thoughts.

Miss Hackett too had stayed back to ponder the morning's events. Especially the interview she'd had with the head nun at half past twelve. Not a very pleasant experience.

"It is my considered opinion Miss Hackett," said Mother Culpertino, "that you have acted unfairly towards Rose O'Brien. Not only had you no shred of evidence, but you failed to take into account the child's honest reputation and tried to humiliate her in front of the class, with that absurd charade about the Black Baby Box!"

"But I tell you Mother, she did take the money. It was gone yesterday afternoon and she was the only person who could have done it!"

"And I tell you, she did not take the money. I've known those O'Brien twins since they were little. They may be somewhat lively, but they are not dishonest. You have only been with us since September and I must assure you, you are deeply mistaken about Rose O'Brien."

Miss Hackett wore a mulish expression of disbelief.

The head nun rose. "If anyone committed the theft then they put the money back before class this morning. It wasn't Rose and there are plenty of witnesses who saw her arrive long after you. You should have questioned other girls in the class and not immediately jumped to conclusions. I don't like to see teachers being unfair. They have so much power. It is essential to use it wisely."

"Herrumph!!" Miss Hackett could not believe her ears. Mother Culpertino was taking the side of that obnoxious child against her. She felt her blood boil, but any further protest was cut off as the head nun bid her good-day and ushered her out the door.

The teacher was raging. Rose O'Brien was going to pay for this! As she corrected copies and prepared work until nearly five o'clock, her mind kept returning to the subject of the Black Baby Box. She brooded resentfully. She had only done her duty reporting the girl to Mother Culpertino. Yet she had been severely reprimanded, while the O'Brien child had got off scot free.

And so Miss Hackett was in much the same frame of mind as Agnes Balfe when they met at the front of the school.

Agnes was still nursing a bloody nose and looking miserable. The woman felt a surge of fondness and concern for her. Now there was a model pupil! She'd never had one ounce of trouble from Agnes Balfe. The child never back-answered, never gave cheek. She could be relied upon to tell Miss Hackett all about the class trouble-makers and would often stay behind to say that so-and-so hadn't got their work done, or someone else had said something awful about the school. She was invaluable. So good and helpful. She put her arm around the large awkward girl.

"Tell me what happened, Agnes." So Agnes told her.

Of course she left out the fact that she had issued the first challenge. And she told Miss Hackett that Rose O'Brien had fought a dirty fight. Cheated like a coward and caused her to crash into a tree.

The teacher's eyes slitted and her nose positively twitched with indignation and sympathy.

"Don't you worry, Agnes. We'll teach that girl a lesson. After robbing the Black Baby money, she deserves everything that's coming to her." Agnes squirmed rather uncomfortably. "I'm not the only teacher who has complaints about her you know. Mrs O'Kelly is most annoyed! Apparently the twins were very rude to her, especially Rose. She must be punished. For her own good of course. Unfortunately Mrs O'Kelly won't be in tomorrow, so we shall have to wait 'til Friday to deal with the matter. Still, that gives us more time to plan, don't you think? Come in early tomorrow morning and we'll talk about it. Rose O'Brien won't get away with it this time!" She squeezed Aggie's shoulder and they went their separate ways, much comforted by the prospect of Rosie's downfall.

At home on Innish Road, Madge and Rosie were making toast at the fire. They held the bread on a fork over the flames and when it had browned on both sides, they buttered it immediately. Rosie knew better now than to ask where the toaster was. Anyway this tasted more delicious than any she'd ever had before. They listened, engrossed, to an adventure on *Children's Hour*. The table was set for tea. Jack came in from football. Granda arrived from work. Rosie put the plateful of buttered toast on the table and Gran brought in a large, deep tart fresh from the oven. It smelled delicious.

"Gurcake," Gran said. "Help yourselves when you've finished your toast and jam."

Help! thought Rosie. I hope this isn't something weird.

Gurcake? What on earth is Gur? Jack was the first to cut himself a hefty piece. Rosie was relieved to see the pastry contained rich layers of fruit. It tasted of delicious spices.

"Yummy!" she said. "Mega Yums!" Madge stared, but Gran looked pleased.

"Yes it turned out nicely. Now eat up."

Rosie decided the first thing she'd do when she got back to her own time was ask Gran to make another Gurcake. It was gorgeous.

"How did you get on at school today Rose?" Granda looked at her over his specs. He reminded her suddenly of Mom when she would lift her head from her corrections. The same quizzical expression. Abruptly, Rosie missed her mother. It wasn't the same at all to have her sitting beside her, aged eleven, in plaits with ribbons. She missed grown-up Mom.

"Well Rose?"

"Oh fine, I got on fine."

"And how was Miss Hackett?" Jack asked meaningfully.

"Very quiet," Rosie smiled. "She was worried about some missing money, but she found it. So everything was alright."

"By the way," Granda said, "I have a wonderful surprise for you lot." They waited eagerly. He looked at Gran. "The boss gave me tickets for the Theatre Royal. For the lot of us. A box! Said it was in appreciation of my hard work over Christmas. He wouldn't have got the new shop finished he said, without the extra time I put into the carpentry. So you better speed up the homework and put on your good clothes. The show starts at eight o'clock."

They got the number 3 bus into town. Rosie felt wonderfully happy. Except of course for the ghastly "Christmas Outfit, 1956" complete with bowler hat.

"We look like mugs in these suits," she whispered to Madge.

"Only men wear suits Rose! Girls wear costumes. We'd look mad altogether if we wore suits." Madge sniggered at the image. But Rosie didn't think they could look much worse.

"A trouser suit would be better than this," she moaned.

"Rose! We'd be taken for lunatics, or part of tonight's panto."

Rosie sighed. Apparently it didn't matter that from the waist up they looked like Charlie Chaplin.

They got into town early and Granda made them get off at Parnell Square to walk the rest of the way.

"Look at O'Connell Street," Rosie gasped. The shops were so different. She stopped at the jewellers next to the Savoy cinema. The window was filled with gold and silver watches. None of them digital. None had calculators, time zones, alarms, memories or games. A shop called Findlaters took the place of the modern office block; Burtons, a "Gentleman's Outfitters", was where The Kylemore café should be, and there were no ugly metal shutters on any of the bright windows.

Her gaze was drawn to the centre of the road. She could not believe it – Nelson's Pillar! Her eyes travelled slowly up the column, past the balcony to the round pedestal on which the proud figure of Nelson stood, his right arm flung wide, surveying the city as if it were his. She wanted to tell them, to shout, "This will be blown up, you know, in 1966." But of course she did not.

Across the wide street she recognised the Carlton cinema, further down were two others she'd never seen before – The Capitol and The Metropole. There were huge queues in front of them and men in long overcoats played the fiddle or the accordion to entertain the crowds.

"Let's go across and look at the *Sunday Press* office," Granda ushered them over. "Be careful of the traffic." There were a few motor vehicles and lots of bicycles. For a child of the nineties, used to thundering lorries, speeding cars, juggernauts, sirens and air-brake-buses, crossing O' Connell Street in 1956 was a doddle.

Outside the *Press* office, on a placard, was the headline:

Cold War goes on
Reds threaten World Peace

They stood alongside an admiring crowd, gazing in the window at a funny looking car, mounted on ramps, cream on the top half, dark brown on the bottom.

"Isn't that Vauxhall beautiful," Granda breathed. "I'd love to win it in the Crossword Competition."

"Can you drive Gra – I mean Da? Have you passed your test?"

"Any man can drive, Rose. You don't need to pass a test!"

"And any woman," Rosie said. "Well, most women," she amended glancing at Madge.

"Maybe so," Granda was doubtful. "I know there are a few lady drivers, but really it's safer to leave it to the men."

Before she could protest they were crossing the street again and making their way to O'Connell Bridge and over to Hawkins Street. Gone were the huge office blocks. Instead Rosie saw the bright lights of the Theatre Royal beside the Regal Rooms cinema. Hundreds of people were heading there. She read the notice:

Commencing December 26th
MOTHER GOOSE
Jack Cruise and Noel Purcell
and All Star Cast

Rosie had never seen anything like it. She had been to most of the theatres in Dublin on her mother's insistence, as part of her education. But this was something else, something special. Inside, it was huge, with ornate boxes and galleries rising one above the other on either side of the stage. There were hundreds of seats at ground floor level, balconies at the back, and the ceiling was almost out of sight. It was breathtaking. Granda led the way through the crowds to the second floor box. Rosie was lost in wonder. In a pit in front of the stage an orchestra played with gusto. The audience shouted and clapped, then settled down as the panto began. Granda produced a great tin of Urney sweets.

Rosie laughed her head off at the corny jokes and silly songs. She loved the dancing girls, the music, the tall white-haired, white bearded man who sang "Dublin can be Heaven" and told ridiculous stories. And she thought the other more blocky man in the loud check jacket and cap was even funnier. She clapped wildly at the end, when the whole cast came onto the stage.

Afterwards they went to Westmoreland Street into the Paradiso Restaurant to "finish off the evening properly." Rosie and Madge had hot chocolate in tall glasses inside silver beakers, sprinkled on top with dark crumbled chocolate. Jack had a huge Banana Split ice cream while the adults ordered coffee and cream. They had a plush booth to themselves. The restaurant was softly lit and a candle flickered on each table lending the evening a magical, unforgettable quality.

"This is the best family outing I've ever had," Rosie thought.

Although they were late home, she made sure to write the day's events in Aunt Rose's diary. She saw with relief that Tuesday was exactly as she had filled it in. Switching her light off, she lay back thinking. Two more days to go. A pity it was impossible to make friends with Agnes Balfe. Then she'd be no further threat. "Well at least I've got

Miss Hackett off my back. She was very quiet today."

Hopefully she would get back to her own time soon. And while she'd be glad to return, she would miss this happy family life. It was great fun having a brother and sister – and a father who came home every evening to ask how you were getting on. And a mother who smiled a lot and was happy.

How everything must have changed after Rose's accident.

She remembered the laughing group they made in the restaurant. If she could alter events, that happiness could last into the future. Her future.

Chapter 10

"I'LL DO it Miss Hackett! There's nothing I'd like better than to get Rose O'Brien into trouble."

Linda Reilly had opened the door to the classroom when she heard Agnes Balfe's voice. She stayed stock still. Something nasty was going on here.

"That girl deserves trouble Agnes. My goodness what a horrible drawing she did of you!" Miss Hackett paused, "And look what she did to your poor face. She must be taught a lesson."

Agnes breathed hard, "Don't you worry Miss Hackett. You just give me Mother Culpertino's purse and I'll slip it into Rose O'Brien's bag at toilet break."

"Excellent Agnes. But you must be very careful no one sees you. Here you are. Now go and sit down. The girls will be coming in soon. That's odd, I thought I closed that door . . . "

Soundlessly Linda made a quick getaway along the corridor. She slipped into the next class. Seeing no one from the doorway, Miss Hackett went back inside.

Wasn't it a good thing, Linda thought, that she had come in early today. Miss Hackett was evil, and Agnes Balfe was her toady. Well they weren't going to get away with this!

At half past ten the class was duly led out to toilet

break. Agnes Balfe was not with them so Linda made sure to be the first to use the toilet. On her way back she saw Agnes at the end of the queue. So! The deed was done. Linda skimmed along the corridor and into the classroom. She knew the rest would take their time in order to postpone lessons as long as possible. Searching through Rose's bag she very quickly found the black purse with its distinctive gold clasp and deposited it deep in Agnes Balfe's bag. Contentedly she sat down.

"I want to enquire Miss Hackett, if anyone has found a black purse with a gold clasp belonging to me?" It was half a hour later and Mother Culpertino had just called in.

"No Mother," said the class.

"Well if any one of you does find it, please come to me immediately. It contains a ten pound note which I'm sure you will agree is quite a lot of money." She turned to go.

"Just a moment Mother Culpertino, your purse may have been robbed!"

The nun frowned. "Well, I did think I'd left it in the drawer of my office, but it's not there, so most likely I'm mistaken."

"I believe, Mother, this could be a robbery and I'm sure none of my girls would mind putting their bags on the desk for you to look through. At least it will eliminate this class."

Mother Culpertino hesitated, but Miss Hackett had already given the order. "Bags on the desks girls. Open up."

Miss Hackett started with great eagerness on Rosie's row, while Mother Culpertino went through the next one. The teacher barely touched Madge's books, but when she came to Rosie's bag she took out every single item.

"She thinks I have it," thought Rosie. "She really is very bad minded." Miss Hackett's face was growing red as she failed to find the purse. Behind her in the other row,

Agnes Balfe insisted on emptying her bag for Mother Culpertino. She even turned it upside down.

In a frenzy, Miss Hackett's hands went through Rosie's books again and again. Nothing! She could not believe it.

"I've found my purse Miss Hackett." Mother Culpertino's voice was quiet, measured. "It was in this girl's bag."

Agnes Balfe was deathly pale. She blurted out, "It's not my fault. It's hers!" pointing at the teacher.

"Yes of course it is Agnes," Miss Hackett said swiftly. "I'm sorry Mother. I gave that purse to Agnes to bring up to your office later, at lunch time. I found it in the corridor on my way in. I'm afraid I didn't make the connection when you said you'd lost your purse. I'm very slow. Silly me!"

There was something fishy going on here, Rosie thought. That was the most feeble excuse she'd ever heard in her life. Mother Culpertino had lost a black purse. Miss Hackett had found one. How could she fail to "make the connection?" And why couldn't she bring it to Mother Culpertino herself instead of giving it to Agnes Balfe? And why was she looking so guilty? It occurred to Rosie that Miss Hackett was off her rocker. Completely mad. It was the only possible explanation.

"Yes. Well, I'm glad I've got my purse back," Mother Culpertino's searching gaze passed from Agnes to Miss Hackett as she left the room.

Linda Reilly hugged herself with glee. That shook those two sneaks! Miss Hackett was furious.

"I gave you a job to do at toilet break Agnes, and you did not do it!" She spoke through gritted teeth.

"I did do it Miss Hackett, I did! I did! I don't know what went wrong. It has to be Rose O'Brien's fault."

"Don't lie to me, girl. I thought I could trust you, but you are obviously just a lazy heap and you can write me an essay on 'Why I am such a Slug'. Five pages please."

Rosie felt sorry for Agnes. Miss Hackett was a horrible woman! No one deserved such insults.

The horrible woman was in a horrible temper. But if she was, Agnes Balfe was a match for her. "If I have to do an essay, I'm going to see Mother Culpertino to explain everything." Her voice was deadly. It had the effect of a bucket of ice-cold water on the teacher's fury. She was visibly shaken.

"On second thought, you need not do the essay. In fact, perhaps, mistakes were made on both sides. I'm sure you're right and someone else is to blame." She looked significantly at Rosie.

The class was totally mystified. This was fascinating stuff but utterly bewildering. They couldn't follow one word of the exchange between Agnes and Miss Hackett, except the bit where Aggie refused to do a punishment essay and got away with it! This only served to confirm Rosie's opinion that Miss Hackett was completely round the bend.

For the second time Miss Hackett was recovering from deep shock. Again she set work for the class while she gazed blankly into space, casting an occasional bitter glance, not just at Rosie this time, but also at Agnes Balfe. She was eager to get rid of them all at dinner time, letting them go a few minutes before the bell rang.

At home Granda was asking them what they'd like to be when they grew up. "I am going to be the most famous dribbler of this century," Jack declared. Rosie stared. What an extraordinary ambition.

"I thought you wanted to be a boxer," said Granda.

"I thought you wanted to be a singer," said Madge.

"I thought you wanted to be a blackmailer," muttered Rosie.

"No. I will be the best dribbler since Stanley Matthews."

Rosie tried to be encouraging. "Well you're not bad at spitting anyway and that's a start." She had seen him win a spitting competition against Eustace Reilly on the way to school, when a great green glob from his mouth landed very impressively on the opposite path. Still, Rosie was somewhat amazed to think dribbling was considered a worthy career in the fifties. Jack was glaring at her. "Spitting indeed! Of course girls know nothing about soccer!"

"I do so! I'm on the school team. How was I to know you meant dribbling a ball?"

Jack shook his head sadly. "Poor deluded girl! On the school team indeed! And I suppose you'll be saying next that a girl can run as fast as Roger Bannister or climb huge mountains like Edmund Hillary!"

Granda cut in, "Never mind him Rose. What would you like to be when you grow up?"

Rosie had no hesitation. "An engineer." Everyone laughed. Rosie was exasperated. "What's the joke?" she demanded.

Jack answered, "You can't do Engineering! It's a man's job, and anyway you have to be really good at Mathematics, not just Sums." Jack was looking smug. "Anyway it's a well known fact that girls are not as good as boys at Sums. Why, in the Inter Cert it's only the girls who do Pass Mathematics – and they don't even have to do it at all if they don't want. No boy can get away with that!"

Rosie felt like hitting Jack. He could be such a pain. But she contented herself with, "That's because it's 1956 and people don't know yet that girls are just as clever as boys. Mom told me all about it."

"Mom?" Jack stared at her.

"I don't remember saying anything of the sort," Gran said. "You're a dreamer Rose, with your 'Mom'. Too many

American comics I think. Though you're right about girls," she sighed. "If only they were given a chance."

"Well things will change. You'll see. And I will be an engineer, Jack. Just like you. My Maths are fine."

Jack snorted, but this time Granda intervened, "And what about you Madge, what do you want to do?"

"I'd like to be a lawyer or join the Gardaí," Madge said firmly.

"You can't be a policeman! That's ridiculous! One sister an engineer and the other a policeman. How would you feel if I wanted to be a nurse?"

"I don't want to be a policeman. I'd be a detective and solve crimes," said Madge.

"And a man could be a nurse!" added Rosie.

"Well a girl can't be a detective," Jack was quite indignant. "As for being a nurse – I'd look silly in a white skirt and hat!"

"Not any sillier than usual," chorused the two girls. They were fed up with Jack.

Rosie was grateful she didn't belong to these mega boring times where a girl could do very little. She turned to Madge, "Would you like to be a teacher?"

"I would not. I want to be a lawyer most of all – or aren't girls allowed to study Law either?" She looked at Gran.

"They are indeed Madge. And maybe you'll be the one to change some laws for women."

Madge looked pleased and said, "I thought you were going to do Law as well Rose. You said we'd work together."

Rosie mumbled something. Gran said they had plenty of time to make up their minds. It was all long years away yet.

"Here's the half crown each for the school photograph," Gran handed them a large silver coin as they left after dinner. "Don't forget to smile. Then you'll have nice photos for your lockets."

As soon as she could, Rosie looked inside the locket. Like her watch, she was still wearing it but had failed to notice until Gran mentioned it. But now the locket was empty and she wondered if her aunt had ever worn it. Maybe she'd been too bitter when she'd come out of hospital to wear anything connected with Madge.

Back in the classroom, the old-fashioned camera was already set up on a tripod. A desk was pushed forward in front of it into which each girl sat in turn and was photographed. On the spur of the moment Rosie whipped off one of the ribbons. Aunt Rose had been wearing two and if she ever saw the photo again, Rosie wanted to be sure who was in it. It might prove it hadn't all been a dream.

Miss Hackett was in a subdued mood and the afternoon passed quietly. On the way home they ran into Mrs O'Kelly. Pursing her lips she looked coldly at both of them. "I have not forgotten your behaviour of yesterday morning. Unfortunately I was not in school today, but tomorrow you will know the consequences of treating me so rudely." She turned on Rosie, "I hear that you in particular, Rose O'Brien, have no respect at all for your teacher. So I have no doubt it was you who roared after me like a vulgar trollop, with the connivance of your sister. Well tomorrow is your day of reckoning my girl."

She strode away and the words echoed in Rosie's fearful heart.

Chapter 11

"MRS REILLY and I are having a cup of tea and a little chat. You won't get anything to eat until six o'clock. So off out with you now and come in when you see your Da." Unceremoniously Gran threw the three of them out of the house.

On the road they were joined by Eustace and Linda. "Our Ma won't let us in 'til she comes home from your place. What'll we do?"

For a while they played marbles along the gutter but soon it was too dark, even in the street light, to see them. Linda brought out two ropes from the side of her house. "French Skipping," she said. Rosie had never heard of it. The two boys held the end of the ropes in each hand. First they swung the right rope in, then the left one. The game was to run in and skip on the two ropes. Linda and Madge managed it beautifully but Rosie got all tangled.

"What's wrong with you Rosie? Thought you were the champion French-Skipper. Stop fooling." Madge was very cross.

"I've lost the knack of it." Rosie was sitting on the ground, practically tied up.

"We'll try one rope then. You take that end Rosie, and

Eustace can take the other. Jack'll go first. Remember, whoever misses a loop or trips on the rope is out and will have to give Eustace a turn."

The game began again and as the rope turned the others began to chant:

"Drip drop, Sailor on the sea
My O my he's calling me
Are you coming to the Fair?
I went and I went, but there was no one there
With your I-must-not-miss-a-Loopio."

This was great fun. They turned the rope faster and faster and it was all the three could do to run in without missing a loop, take a skip and dash round to start again. First Linda was out, then Jack. Rosie soon got the hang of the weird chants . . .

"Vote vote vote for Dev-a-lera
In comes Cosgrave at the door-i-o
Now we'll have a bit of fun
And we'll vote the other one
So we won't have Dev any more-i-o"

But the marvellous game ended with one of Jack's great ideas. "Let's play Nik-Nak," he said, pulling a ball of grubby string from his pocket. "This is long enough to do the Fahy's door and Father Meaney's." They gasped at the daring of it.

"Father Meany'll kill us!"

"He won't know what's happening. We've never done it before on him. Or on Mrs Fahy. They're both so cross. It'd be great fun. Come on! Let's try it." He was very persuasive. He broke off a huge length of string.

"This should be enough." He took one end and Madge

grabbed the other. Expertly they tied them around the adjoining knockers. Back on the road, Jack gave a few hefty tugs. The string was thin but strong and the knocks were very loud. When the lights went on in the hallways, Jack let the string drop and they retreated to the shadow of a tree, well away from the street light.

"What's all this racket? Hey! Who have we here? No one!" It was Father Meany. He walked out into the garden and stood near his neighbour's railing. Mrs Fahy opened her door a second later and stepped out.

"Hello Father Meany," her voice was puzzled.

"Good evening Mrs Fahy." Both hesitated a moment and went back in.

A few minutes later the loud knocking started again. Father Meany was out first, standing in his garden, looking up and down. He could see no-one. Mrs Fahy reappeared. She looked at the priest thoughtfully.

"Is there something we want Mrs Fahy? Something on my person we greatly desire? We seem to be displaying huge curiosity in this direction!" Father Meany was extremely irate.

The group under the tree giggled.

"No Father! And I hope you're not doing it!" Mrs Fahy snapped back and went in slamming the door. In a few minutes Father Meany followed suit. This time, when the knocking started, the children barely had time to rush into the shadows before Father Meany thundered into the garden. Mrs Fahy was only seconds behind. She exploded, "How dare you Father Meany! Such silly behaviour! You need a doctor!"

"I need a doctor! It's we who need medical attention. Every time I come out here my good woman, we open our door to stare at me. Of course everyone knows how nosy we are. Infernal busybody."

"You are daft in the head Father Meany. A man of your

age and a priest too! Well I'll not open this door again, I can tell you! Not to listen to such Gobbledegook!" She flounced in.

"I'm very glad to hear it! At least we won't be watching my every move!" Father Meany was yelling so loudly a few other doors opened. He hastily took himself in.

"Now's the time to give up," Jack whispered. They waited five minutes. Then the two swiftly undid the string again. They had got away with it!

There was at least half an hour before going in and Linda suggested a trip round to the shops to spend the two pennies she still had from her pocket-money.

Outside Morgan's shop they met Agnes Balfe and her brother Mel.

"There's that dope Rose O'Brien. She can't do even the simplest sum," Agnes proclaimed loudly.

Rosie was quite happy to ignore her, but of course Madge had to interfere.

"Our Rose is great at sums. She gets first in every test — except the last one."

"Only because she copies. And she got nought in the last one. I suppose that's a sign of genius!"

"She just had a bad day," Madge declared stoutly, while Rosie tried to hush her up.

Agnes's brother Mel entered the battle. "You O'Briens think your it! An' you're a real teacher's pet Jack O'Brien, with your 'Yes Sir, no Sir! Three bags full Sir!' Everyone knows he gives you all the easy questions. And everyone knows the O'Briens are as thick as semolina!"

Jack felt obliged to defend the family honour. "You give us any sum and we'll do it in our heads — any sum at all." He waited confidently.

"Any sum?" Agnes Balfe's eyes glistened in the light from the shop.

"Except one with money," Rose said.

"You said you could do any sum!"

"Not one with money," Rosie said firmly. "But we'll add, subtract, multiply and divide any figures in less than one minute."

"Hang on," Jack muttered "I don't think we can do that."

"Yes we can!" Rosie was definite. Her confidence seemed to enrage Agnes.

"Right Miss Smartie Pants. Try this: 214 + 371 + 633." She began to jot down the figures herself with the butt of a pencil and a scrap of paper she had in her pocket.

"1218," Rosie declared promptly.

Aggie's mouth was open – as was everyone else's. "You're making it up," she said furiously.

"I am not. Add them up." It took Agnes a few minutes to tot up the figures. She was madder than ever.

"Okay Miss Know-All. Here's another one. Fifty-four multiplied by sixty-eight."

"3672," Rosie said while Agnes was still writing down the sum.

Again it was right.

"You're a genius Rose," Madge declared proudly.

"That was cinchy," Agnes Balfe sneered. "Bet you can't do this one – hang on 'til I write it down first."

While they waited Jack said admiringly, "I take it all back Rose. You're better than any boy at sums."

But Rosie hadn't the time to bask in his praise.

"Get round me in a circle so she can't see what I'm doing," she told the others hastily. Mystified, they did so.

Then Agnes called out, "314 - 72 x 66 + 93 divided by 15 x 41."

Quickly Rosie again worked the calculator watch. The others watched mesmerised.

"43,911" Rosie said calmly almost as soon as Agnes finished calling out the numbers.

This time it took Agnes ten minutes to work it out.

"You're wrong Smartie Fartie!" she sneered with glee. "The answer is 43,811."

"I am not wrong. You're wrong. Work it out again."

Seething Aggie did so again, but she was wrong and that horrible little louse was right. She crumpled up the paper. "I can't be bothered with this stupid game," she said. "You'll get what's coming to you tomorrow Rose O'Brien."

"Teacher's Door Mat!" her brother yelled at Jack.

"Ah go home and have a good wash Smelly Melly," Jack taunted. But the two Balfes were already on their way. They'd had enough.

"Let's see how you did that Rose. What are you wearing on your wrist?"

Rosie showed them. She showed them how the calculator worked, the time zones, the memory for dates and the alarm.

"The time on it is very odd," Madge said. "What's 17:45?" Rosie explained the twenty-four hour clock. They looked at her with great respect. Jack couldn't get over the magic. A watch that could remember birthdays, do all your hard sums and tell you the time in Tokyo and New York!

"It's massive Rose," he sighed enviously. "Where did you get it? It's like something from the future."

For a split second Rosie hesitated. Would she tell them? Jack noticed her sudden thoughtfulness and watched her keenly. But she couldn't. They could not possibly believe her and she'd never convince them. Reluctantly she took the easy way out.

"Oh, I found it the other night in O'Connell Street. I wanted to surprise you with it, but I didn't think it would be Agnes Balfe who'd give me the chance."

"It must be worth a fortune Rose. You'll have to give it

up at a police station," said Madge.

But Jack said carefully, "If it was worth a fortune we'd have read about it in the *Press*. It would be reported as missing. I'd say it belonged to a foreigner, American or Japanese, and they've gone home by now."

He watched Rosie and noticed she seemed relieved at this explanation. He began to wonder. Really she was behaving very oddly these days. She didn't seem to understand half of what was going on. Imagine thinking Bill Haley was old fashioned! And how did she know all those things about the watch if she found it in O' Connell Street? She'd have to be a genius. He gazed at her, considering.

"You know Jack, you think more of this old watch than I do." She smiled at him. "Why don't you take it?" She slipped it off. She had never seen him speechless before. Taking his hand, she put the watch into it. She might have been handing him a million pounds.

"Gosh. Rose. This is . . . Are you sure?"

She nodded.

"Yippee! Yippee-i-o!" Jack whooped around the pavement. "Yahoo! Wait 'til everyone sees this in school tomorrow. You're. You're massive!"

"I am not massive, I'm normal size," but she smiled at the compliment. "Better not tell Ma or Da about it though. They might make you hand it in." Jack couldn't get over his good fortune and did a giddy gallop around them. Linda went into Morgan's and got twenty Nancy Balls, five each. Rosie sucked the tiny sweets. Delicious aniseed taste.

"You certainly showed those Mouldy Balfes," Eustace said happily. A great contentment settled on the group until Jack looked at his new watch.

"Hey, its eighteen hundred hours! Six o'clock. We'll be late for tea." They all ran.

Later, after homework, the family settled around the fire to listen to *Smash Hits* on Radio Luxembourg. Someone called Cyril Stapleton and his Orchestra were playing "Blue Star" over the air waves.

I won't be sorry to leave them behind, Rosie thought. A song followed about a fella who wanted a China Doll instead of a girlfriend. "She'll never leave me, She'll not deceive me Nor ever grie–ieve me, My china doll." Very weird. Imagine a grown man bringing a doll to the pictures. Rosie giggled to herself. If only they could see Sinéad O'Connor! I wonder what they'd think?

This was possibly her last night in 1956. She was glad she'd met Granda. Looking at him now, reading a book and half listening to the radio, Rosie thought how nice he was. And how different Madge was to Mom. Playing Nik-Nak, roaring at Mrs O'Kelly – she wasn't half so serious as her grown-up self. Though Jack, with his great ideas and marvellous energy would not become too different. Except of course, he'd change his mind about girls being inferior to boys. He'd realise girls could do sums just as well as any boy. Especially when his own daughter was a wizard at Maths.

And Gran, like Madge, would grow sadder and more thoughtful.

As for school! How different things were in 1956. Teachers waiting for a chance to use the cane! Miss Hackett was a witch trying to cast a spell of misery over the class. And Rosie knew Agnes Balfe wanted to destroy her.

Like a sudden knife-thrust Mrs O'Kelly's words struck her: "Tomorrow is your Day of reckoning!"

Rosie had a terrible sense of dread. Later in the diary she echoed her aunt's last entry:

Tomorrow is Friday 13th, something awful may happen. Perhaps I won't be able to change anything. Perhaps I won't get back to the 1990's.

That night she dreamed of darkness. A figure flew at her like a bat out of hell and a voice cackled, "Your Day of Reckoning!"

Agnes Balfe's face loomed at her. Miss Hackett grinned evilly and shook a box in her face. Mrs O'Kelly pointed at something in the distance. Rosie's terrified gaze followed the menacing finger.

A small figure on a swing was creaking backward and forward in an empty playground.

Chapter 12

ON THAT last day, Friday 13th January, 1956, Dublin was shrouded in heavy fog. It lay like a pall on the city. People moved like ghosts, looming suddenly into view, only to vanish a few moments later. Traffic was muffled and voices hushed. Everywhere activity was cloaked in a thick grey swirl. That evening the headlines in Granda's paper would shout:

Fog Hits City

A photograph would show O'Connell Bridge at eleven am, barely visible in the gloom, the street lights casting an eerie glow on the shadowy passers-by.

But Rosie would never see the *Evening Press* that night. For her Destiny waited in an afternoon playground.

Now at breakfast, she sat silent and sad, unable to eat.

"Are you sick Rose? You look very pale. Perhaps you shouldn't go to school?" Gran was concerned.

Was this a way out?

Rosie considered carefully. If she avoided school she wouldn't meet Agnes Balfe and nothing would happen to her. But that would mean she'd be stuck in 1956! And what about Aunt Rose? Rosie did not believe she could change things for the better by trying to avoid Fate. In the end a plea from Madge made up her mind.

"Come to school Rose, please. I don't want to face Mrs O'Kelly on my own."

"You should never have roared 'Smelly O'Kelly' after her."

"Oh God, I didn't really say that, did I?"

"You certainly did. You said she ponged like a Welly."

"Ah no. I couldn't have. I wouldn't have . . . Maybe she didn't hear me properly?"

"Everyone heard you. With your voice, you'd get a job as a foghorn. Very useful in this weather."

"I'm sure you're wrong. She couldn't have heard the exact words."

"Of course she could. I'm telling you! You could be heard a mile away. Kids rushed out their doors when you roared."

Madge stared at her in consternation. Then she relaxed. "That's because they were going to school, Nasty!"

"Anyway why are you worried? It's me she's blaming."

"Because I'll have to tell her it was me. It'd be much easier though, if you were there." Madge needed her support and how could she refuse?

So in the end, in an odd kind of way, it was her Mom who sealed Rosie's fate.

Reluctantly she got up to go, assuring Gran she was fine. At the last minute Madge ran upstairs to look for a mislaid copy. Rosie dragged her feet up the street. Jack came with her as far as the corner. "What's the matter Rose? You look like a ghost."

Rosie shivered. "Nothing," she muttered.

"Is it Agnes Balfe? Is she still out to get you?"

And she confided in him, "I think she might have something drastic planned for today."

"Like what?"

"I don't know . . . She might try to get me to do the High Swing Challenge."

"Well everyone does that sometime. Why are you afraid?"

"I might be badly hurt . . . Or even killed."

He stared at her. "You'd be the first so! How could you get killed? It's not like you to be chicken over a swing Rose!"

"Well something terrible has to happen today. Otherwise how will I get back?" As soon as she spoke, Rosie knew she had said too much.

Jack pounced. "Get back where?"

"Get back nowhere. Get back at Agnes Balfe for all the aggro she's caused."

"You're not making sense Rose. One minute you're afraid of Aggie, next you want to get back at her. And what's this 'Ah grow?' You speak a different language half the time. 'Time Zones', 'Mega', 'Deadly'. Very strange."

Rosie knew what he meant. He was sometimes hard to understand too.

"And how do you know so much about the watch," he went on, "if you just found it in the street? I've never heard of a watch like it, but you knew which button to press and exactly what it could do. What's going on Rose?"

She said nothing. At that moment Madge caught up on them and urged Rosie to hurry. She needed no second bidding, but zoomed off, leaving Jack staring after her, scratching his head.

"Now girls, go over all the spellings in your Reader from pages twenty to forty for fifteen minutes. Then I'll give you a test."

Another flamin' test! And she'd never even told them yesterday. Aunt Rose would certainly fail. Maybe she should change that! Rosie's eyes narrowed.

When the time was up Miss Hackett looked at Rosie malevolently. "And just to make sure you don't copy Miss Rose O'Brien, you can come up to my desk and do the test on your own."

Sighing, Rosie did as she was told. Miss Hackett swung her own chair around to the side of the platform for her. A little steel entered Rosie's nerves. She was damned if she was going to deliberately misspell this test. It was her last day anyway. So what did it matter what Miss Hackett thought of her. For never in her wildest imaginings would the teacher hit on the truth.

Then Miss Hackett made a point of taking away Rosie's book. She flicked through her copy to make sure the spellings weren't already written inside. "Now empty your pockets, you might have a list hidden," Rosie shrugged and pulled out her empty pockets. It was obvious she couldn't have written twenty pages of words in a quarter of an hour. Miss Hackett was just being spiteful. She stood facing the class on her platform, almost breathing down Rosie's neck, to give an impression of complete distrust.

She called out fifty words. Some of them were very difficult such as "excruciating", "sensitivity", and "violin concerto". She trained her beady eyes on Rosie, waiting for her to give up, as Aunt Rose had given up so often in the past. But Rosie kept her head down and diligently wrote each word as it was called. Miss Hackett sneered, "I do hope I can make out your words Rose O'Brien. Last time you wrote s-c-r-e-w-t-i-n-n-e-y-e-s for 'scrutinise'." The class sniggered. Rose O'Brien's spelling was notorious.

Miss Hackett collected all the tests, leaving Rosie's till last, so it would be first corrected. The sooner the fun started at this obnoxious girl's expense the better!

She held the pen with relish, ready to slash through the paper. But it remained poised above the page while her mouth dropped. She went through Rosie's test at least three times. When she had finished with it she slammed it down, corrected the others and gave the lot to Linda to hand back.

Rosie scored forty-nine marks out of fifty. First in the class! Madge got forty-six, the same as Agnes Balfe. The news of Rose O'Brien's first place in Spelling spread like wildfire. Nobody could understand it. Up to today she had been the worst speller on the face of the earth, now she was the best in the class! And Miss Hackett had gone out of her way to make sure she didn't copy.

So! She had done it all on her own. Mystified, everyone stared at her. The teacher ground her teeth. Rosie sat there grinning delightedly. She had beaten Miss Hackett – and she'd outscored Mom!

When Madge mentioned Rosie's marvellous Spelling test at dinner time, the family was equally bewildered.

"But Rose, you can't spell. You never could spell. How could you score forty-nine?" Gran asked. Granda thought it was a miracle.

Jack looked thoughtful. "Very strange," he said.

But Rosie was still on a high from the effect she'd had on the class that morning. Even Agnes Balfe had looked at her in awe. And no wonder. To judge from the journal, Aunt Rose's spelling was, at the very least, unique. And now suddenly she could spell far better than everyone else. Rosie giggled.

"I think there's something wrong with Rose," Jack said suddenly, "Maybe she should see a doctor, Ma."

"Why?" Gran was astonished.

"Because she's acting peculiar. She can't become a perfect speller overnight!"

"I can't bring her to the doctor and say she's got perfect spelling wrong with her. That's not a disease. He'd lock me up for being daft."

But Jack persisted, "Maybe she should take a tonic or more cod-liver oil or something. Then she'd be her old self."

More cod liver oil! Rosie stopped smiling.

"Have a bit of sense son," Granda said gruffly. "Why should she want to be her old self? What's wrong with her new self and perfect spelling?"

But Jack didn't really know what was wrong. It was just a feeling he had. And since he couldn't put it into words he subsided.

Later he took Rosie aside. "Listen I was thinking about what you said this morning. If Agnes Balfe tries any funny stuff, just run off. If she dares you to try the High Swing Challenge don't listen to her."

"Why have you changed your mind?"

"I just have an odd notion about today. Maybe it's because it's Friday the 13th," he said.

"I will tackle those girls, Miss Hackett, when the whole class is seated." Mrs O'Kelly was already in the room when they arrived back after dinner. Rosie's heart sank. She had made herself believe when the mean teacher hadn't appeared that morning she was not going to appear at all. Looking at the grim figure with the tightly permed hair and the pursed lips, Rosie could easily imagine her taking a prim delight in confiscating Madge's Nancy Balls.

The class sat in expectant silence. Really life had been very eventful since they'd come back after Christmas! At least one crisis a day. What drama could unfold now?

Mrs O'Kelly turned to Miss Hackett. "I have a most grievous complaint to make about two girls in this class. Two common hooligans. One of them, aided and abetted by the other, roared the rudest of rude rhymes after me. And on the public highway too."

Fifty-four young faces looked around eagerly to see who

the culprits were. The twins stared straight ahead. Miss Hackett was in her element. "Would those two HARRIDANS stand up IMMEDIATELY!"

Rosie didn't know what a harridan was, nevertheless, she stood up promptly. So did Madge.

Mrs O'Kelly pointed an accusing and dramatic finger at them, as if no-one could possibly see them otherwise. "It was you, Rose O'Brien, who behaved like a guttersnipe!"

Then Miss Hackett seized the opportunity to embarrass Rosie.

"Repeat the rhyme girl." she ordered.

It was Mrs O'Kelly who blushed. "I really don't think that's absolutely necess . . . "

"Of course it is! The class must realise what is acceptable behaviour and what is not. Do as I say girl."

Rosie obliged quite happily. The rhyme had stayed in her head over the last couple of days and she'd made some improvements.

"Mrs O'Kelly's very smelly
Smelly like a sour old welly,
The pong is like a Stinky Cheetah
When her socks are off her feetah
And what nearly stops your heart,
Is the whiff of . . . "

"Rose O' Brien! Stop that at once!"

"Her Apple Tart!" Rosie finished triumphantly. She spoke loud and clear in ringing tones. There was a collective gasp and the class nearly passed out at her daring. The two adults were gobsmacked. But of course they did not stay that way for long.

"Trollop!" hissed Miss Hackett.

"Vile Vulgarian!" snarled Mrs O'Kelly.

Funny how they don't mind calling me names, thought Rosie indignantly.

The two teachers went into a huddle. Then Mrs O'Kelly announced, "I will leave this matter to your teacher. Suffice it to say I have never been so ridiculed in all my life!" She flounced out of the room.

Madge tried to tell Miss Hackett it wasn't her sister's fault, that she had started it all.

"Fine, Madge O'Brien! You can do a ten page composition for trying to protect that terrible hussy. Call it 'Good Manners and Name Calling'." Her eyes gleamed. "Now you, Rose O'Brien! Come up here." She really was extremely rude. She had absolutely no respect for any of the girls in her class, not even for Agnes Balfe.

Rosie McGrath was not going to take it anymore. Miss Hackett did not deserve politeness. She had pulled her around the room, caned her, put a Donkey's Tail on her, called her a clot, an eejit, a trollop and heaven knows what else! Rosie was about to get her revenge.

She swaggered up to the platform, chewing a bit of pencil wood as though it were gum, making sure her lip curled in a sneer. She stared insolently at Miss Hackett who was purple with fury.

"How dare you behave like a gurrier! Spit out whatever you're chewing." Of course she expected Rosie to use the waste-paper basket, but she never said so. Rosie spat the slivers on to Miss Hackett's table.

Madge groaned and put her head on the desk. She didn't want to witness the slaughter.

Rosie beamed at her classmates while the teacher grabbed the cane. "You'll wear the Donkey's Tail for two weeks and sit in the Dunces row 'til summer. Now you will put out your hand and I will give you such a beating you will never forget it!" She was spitting out the words.

Rosie shrugged her shoulders and casually held out her

hand, waving first at Linda, who almost had a heart attack.

Miss Hackett raised the cane high above her shoulder and brought it down with full force. But Rosie's hand was no longer there. Neither was Rosie. She was already at the door. "Rotten Old Witch!" she shouted, as the teacher tottered over from the strength of the would-be blow. "Flamin' Monster! You should be locked up for life with a Donkey's Tail pinned to your bum!"

Then she was gone, leaving class and teacher shell-shocked.

Chapter 13

"AUNT ROSE you must help me! You must come back," Rosie prayed as she ran like the wind down the corridor, out the main door and through the yard. At the school gate she stopped. The fog swirled around her. She was out of breath, almost bent double from the desperate sprint. "I've never behaved so badly in all my life," she thought.

But then no one had ever treated her like Miss Hackett.

She thought of Stormin' Norman and all the prizes he gave out: for work, sport, for punctuality – for lots of things. He made sure everyone got a prize. In his eyes each person was good at something. Okay, he was a grump sometimes when you didn't do your best. Sometimes a mega grump, maybe even a gross grump! But he tried to be fair. He didn't run the class like a prison camp.

Rosie suddenly wished she could see Mom, as Mom of course, not as some crazy eleven year old who caused terrible trouble with her rhymes.

She leaned against the school gate, "You've got to come back Aunt Rose," she whispered. "I can't stand it here."

Suddenly a reassuring voice was in her head. "It won't be long now Rosie. Just don't accept the High Swing

Challenge. No matter what happens. Do as I say and we'll see each other soon."

Rosie closed her eyes and focussed her mind on the voice in her head. "I could just go home," she suggested.

"If you do that you'll have to stay here as Rose O'Brien. Rosie McGrath will have no future."

"And what about you. What would happen to you Aunt Rose?"

"You'd be me. I'd fade away as if I'd never existed."

Rosie considered. There was no way out. "What if I take the Challenge? I could still change events. I don't have to wave like you did. You should never have let go."

The voice sighed. "I don't think it will make any difference, Rosie. That swing went so high I was thrown backwards, and lost my balance."

"So if I take the Challenge I'll have the same accident as you?"

"Yes."

There was a silence and then the voice spoke again. "You must change the past Rosie. Get rid of all that bitterness waiting for Madge and me. Our future depends on what happens next. Very few of us are given the opportunity to change lives. This is your chance – and my hope."

But Rosie was afraid. If she went to the playground on this ominous day, wasn't she going along with Rose's fate? In her mind's eye she could see what would happen. Agnes Balfe, herself and Madge, like figures in a ritual dance, or actors in a play, the parts and movements had been written long ago. A challenge issued and the plot set in motion.

Had she the strength to alter such powerful forces?

"All you have to do is refuse the Challenge no matter what happens." The voice was fading in an echo. "No matter what happens Rosie."

So. There was no way out.

No point in going home then. Anyway Gran would ask too many questions. Why was she home so early? Where was her bag? Her coat? She would've liked to say goodbye to Granda, but that was impossible.

No point in hanging around the school either. She might be spotted and marched back. She could wait for Madge in the playground.

Rosie was freezing. The fog was damp and enveloped her as she swayed gently on a swing. Perhaps she would die of pneumonia. That would be one way of solving her problems.

After four o'clock the children began drifting home from school. In the dense mist they really were like ghosts from the past.

"Rose, is that you on the swing?" It was Linda Reilly. She stood with a group of shadows peering into the playground. Rosie didn't answer. She did not want to talk to them about what had happened. They had been so horrified. She would never have spoken to Stormin' Norman like that. Not in a million years. But she didn't belong to this time and probably wouldn't have to face the consequences. Linda Reilly and the others were trapped here and it would only make things worse for them if they rebelled against Miss Hackett and took her side.

"Rose, is that you?" Linda separated from the group and came over. "Howya," she smiled, then went on in a rush. "You were great! You should have seen Miss Hackett's face after you left. She went boiling red, then purple and then dead white. She nearly fainted, Rose. She went to sit down, but the chair wasn't there and she sat on the floor instead." Linda looked at Rosie and giggled. In her present state it didn't take much to make Rosie hysterical. She pictured Miss Hackett disappearing behind her desk and sitting abruptly on the floor. She began to laugh and in a moment the two girls were in fits. She stood up clutching the rope of the swing. Linda leaned against her while they wept with merriment.

Madge struggled into the playground, through the group at the entrance, carrying two school bags and an extra coat. The fog cleared for a moment and Rosie saw the hot and bothered figure staring at her grimly.

"You're to be expelled!" Madge announced. "Miss Hackett said."

This did not have the sobering effect she intended. Instead of a wail of anguish, Rosie doubled up completely and howled with laughter. After a shocked second, Linda too fell around.

"This is serious. Da will kill you Rose!"

Rosie gulped for breath and began to recover, until she looked at Madge's cross face and then she started all over again.

But suddenly Madge was pushed aside and Agnes Balfe stood there, stocky, rough, glaring at Rose.

"Show off," she hissed "Think you're wonderful talking to Miss Hackett like that. But you're not so brave are you! There's one thing you're afraid of, isn't there? Chicken!" She pushed her face close to Rosie's, her expression fierce. Still in an hysterical mood Rosie thought the large looming girl was ridiculous. The glowering face sent her off once more into a fit of giggles.

Agnes Balfe began to feel silly. Linda laughed scornfully. The crowd behind sniggered. The class bully might have sneaked off if Madge hadn't interfered.

"Who do you think you are Agnes Balfe? Calling my sister chicken. And who do you think you are Rose, laughing at everything?"

Rosie recovered sufficiently to say in a fit of madness, "Who do I think I am? I know who I am! I'm Rosie McGrath, not Rose O'Brien! I'm your daughter, not your sister."

Oh God! What had she said? She sobered up immediately. Madge was furious. Boiling.

"Jack was right when he said you ought to see a doctor! Because what you are, Rose O'Brien, is a complete and utter lunatic." She was bawling the words. "And it is just my luck to have a raving loony for a twin."

Rosie was highly indignant. Raving loony indeed!

"I wasn't the raving loony who started all the trouble," she yelled at Madge. "I didn't roar at Mrs O'Kelly in the street."

"No. You roared at her in the class instead! Your rhyme was a lot ruder than mine. It wasn't bravery. It was madness."

Agnes Balfe was delighted.

"I do think you're right Madge," she said sweetly, "your sister is insane. Does it run in the family? Your brother doesn't seem quite right in the head either, it's very sad."

"Shut up. I don't need your sympathy you Big Bully." Madge was raging.

Agnes Balfe got mad again. "Not only is your twin bonkers," she said, "she is also a rotten coward."

Fiercely Madge turned on her. "What are you talking about? My sister's no coward. You saw her yourself with Miss Hackett."

"Huh. She's the biggest chicken in the world. She won't take the High Swing Challenge. She's terrified. Look at her." Indeed Rosie had paled and bowed her head.

"Of course she will. She's not afraid . . . Are you Rose?" Madge was pleading with her not to let her down.

Rosie said, "We don't have anything to prove to her, Madge. Any sum she asked us we could do! I even beat her in the Spelling test. She won't stop at the High Swing Challenge." She turned on the menacing girl. "You'll just go on and on looking for revenge. You can't be a good loser, can you?"

For a moment Agnes looked uncertain, losing some of her aggression. Rosie saw her chance. "You don't have to hate me Agnes. We could try to be friends. I don't hate you." Her voice rang with sincerity. She really did not hate the other girl. If anything she felt sorry for her. And now everything depended on convincing her they didn't have to be mortal enemies.

Agnes wavered. For a moment she saw the possibilities. With Rose O'Brien for a friend, she'd no longer be the outsider. Never again would she have to be tough and mean to make her presence felt. Instead of destroying the schoolyard games, she could join in. Earn a cheer and a friendly word instead of hostile whispers. Agnes's eyes began to light up at the prospect and she almost smiled at Rosie. Then one of the crowd destroyed it all.

"Why be nice to her Rose? She's a big bully. Just like your drawing!" A snigger ran around the playground.

A wave of shame swept over Agnes. That drawing was how Rose O'Brien really saw her! How could she be friends with someone who thought she was as rotten as that picture. A cold determination gripped her. She would destroy her enemy now.

"Be friends with you Rose O'Brien? Not on your life! You let your friends down. Look at you! Everyone here – they're all your pals. They want to see you take the Challenge. But you're too much of a coward."

The crowd was indignant.

"Don't let her talk to you like that Rose."

"Show her who's best."

"Aggie the Haggie . . . "

The crowd took up the chant, "Aggie the Haggie . . . Aggie the Haggie . . . "

No peace was possible now.

Rosie waited.

A silence descended gradually. Madge, Linda and her classmates looked confidently at her. Their heroine. How could she let them down?

But Aunt Rose's words came unbidden, loud and clear. "Don't accept the High Swing Challenge – no matter what happens."

The words echoed in her head. She knew quite clearly she would never change things for Madge and Rose if she did. Quietly she said, "I'm not going to let you push me on that swing Agnes Balfe. It's too dangerous. And how can you say I'm a coward? I took you on in a fight and I beat you, even though you're much bigger than me."

"That's right Rose," said Linda "You're no coward. You don't have to prove anything." But the rest of the group remained silent. Like Madge, they were disappointed.

"You did not beat me in the fight," Agnes Balfe felt goaded now. "You never even hurt me. It was your sneaky tricks that beat me. In a fair fight I'd squash you like the worm you are. But your slimy ways won't help with the High Swing Challenge, will they? No! You're just a yellow chicken!"

"Go on, Rose."

"You show her!"

"Don't let Aggie the Hag win!"

The encouragement came in a heady wave.

"Hurry up Rose. Just do it." It was Madge.

"No I won't," Rosie said fiercely and began to walk away.

"Right. I'll go on the swing Agnes Balfe. You can push me as high as you like!" Madge shouted the words at Rosie's retreating back. She whirled around. This was awful. If Madge – Mom – took the Challenge – if she went into a coma . . . why maybe she'd go to America at seventeen and never meet Dad and she, Rosie, would never exist. And what about Aunt Rose? Her head was splitting in the effort to grasp all the consequences of Madge's careless words.

"I don't care which of you takes the challenge." Agnes Balfe was triumphant. Evil. Madge was already sitting on the swing.

Rosie rushed over, grabbed her arm and dragged her off. Raging, Madge pushed her away and tried to get back on. Rosie grappled with her. They struggled for possession.

She heard Agnes Balfe's gleeful laugh. She didn't care. Holding Madge off with one hand, she managed to push the swing high in the air with the other. Then she tried to pull Madge away. But red faced with anger Madge wouldn't budge. Instead she seized Rosie by the shoulders and swung her around, shaking her furiously and when the swing hurtled back down it cracked against the back of Rosie's head. She saw Madge's dismayed face, then everything went black.

What she never saw was the panic that followed.

Madge was down at her side begging, "Say something Rose, please please say something!"

Linda Reilly raced out of the playground in one direction.

Agnes Balfe rushed off in another.

Linda was running for Mrs O'Brien and Agnes was running away, witless with fear.

Madge made a pillow of Rosie's bag and settled it under her head. She covered her gently with her coat.

In the dense fog they stood, a silent ring around the still form.

Soon Gran came rushing into the playground. When Linda had told her the awful news, she had run out of the house just as she was, still wearing her slippers and apron. She knelt beside Rosie, gripping her hand. "Dear God in Heaven! Is she dead?"

Madge shook her head helplessly. She did not know.

Linda came running, "Father Meany is phoning for an ambulance," she told them.

But Rosie never woke up to see the arrival of the ambulance. The fog parted its thickness for the stretcher bearers. Gran and Madge went with her. Silently the crowd dispersed into the shadows.

And then the freezing fog surged back into the playground as the ambulance wailed off into the distance.

Chapter 14

I T WAS pitch black for a long time. Silent as the grave. Rosie found the darkness restful, a cocoon of peace. A gentle safe haven. She could have stayed there for always. Yet she had a sense of lingering, of resting on the edge. Her mind contemplated the past, the present and forever, and waited tranquilly for some kind of message.

After what seemed an eternity it came. A faint voice, travelling through the years, calling to the deep recesses of her soul:

"Rosie . . . Rosie . . . wake up . . . "

Would she answer or choose the comfort of darkness and never-ending sleep? She was tempted and stayed still, quiet, unwilling to be disturbed. It would be so easy to slip away.

"Rosie! Please Please wake up!"

It was Mom. Not the unpredictable mischievous eleven year old, but her real Mom, safe and solid, and right now Rosie wanted her.

Her eyelids fluttered and turning towards the voice, she took in the white hospital room, the machine beside the bed, the array of tubes and wires, the mask over her face. The moment she moved, she knew her head was swathed in bandages.

"Rosie . . . " Madge looked as if the sun had begun to

shine after a long black night. She was smiling tearfully. "About time too. Nearly five days you've been unconscious. We were worried sick."

Beneath the mask Rosie smiled. She was back! Free of the past! But had it been worthwhile? Did she manage to change things? She had to know. Madge sensed her agitation.

"Don't try to talk. The doctor said you were to keep calm. Any excitement could cause a relapse!"

Did that mean she could end up in 1956 again?

"No thank you!" Rosie thought "I'd hate another meeting with Miss Hackett and Agnes Balfe. Rotweillers have more charm than that flamin' pair!" So she smiled at Mom and relaxed. Questions could wait.

One afternoon, less than a week later she was sitting up in bed free of masks and tubes and so well on her way to recovery that Mom obviously felt she was able to handle some good news.

"You won't believe what happened!" she said.

"Is it Aunt Rose? You're friends again! So I did change things!"

"How on earth did you guess? When you were knocked down Gran phoned her and told her you were seriously ill. She thought Rose would be polite and cool the way she always is where I'm concerned. But not this time. Gran said she got very upset and couldn't talk. Then a few days ago I got this from her."

Mom rummaged in her bag, unfolded a letter and handed it to Rosie. "If it weren't for you she wouldn't have contacted me. See for yourself."

Staring at the neat pages Rosie said, "Why does she always type her letters?"

"Because she's the worst speller on the face of the earth and the spell-check on her word processor corrects all her mistakes. Though I'm surprised it hasn't broken down with nervous exhaustion!" Rosie read:

> Dear Madge,
>
> It's wonderful to hear that Rosie is getting better. The worry must have been unbearable.
>
> When Mother told me what happened it took me back all those years to my own accident. After that phone-call I spent hours thinking about us and realised you and I should have talked long ago.
>
> You remember how inseparable we were as children? How we did everything together and stuck up for one another against Agnes Balfe and that teacher – Miss Whatsername? They were great times. Then suddenly you weren't there any more; you didn't want to see me and I couldn't understand your reasons.
>
> Sometimes Mother can be very direct. She told me I should stop being so selfish, that although I hadn't died you'd lost me anyhow and now you might lose Rosie too. I thought how I'd react if anything happened to Hattie or Shane and suddenly realised how you'd felt over me.
>
> I never opened any of your letters, but neither could I throw them out and after Mother's call I went through every one of them. I see now it is you who have kept the faith across the years and I who let you down. So, Madge, I'm coming home. Henry has been urging me for ages to make the trip and rushed out to buy four tickets the minute I suggested it. We're dropping everything and leaving almost immediately. I can't believe I've wasted all this time. Give my love to Rosie and tell her Shane and Hattie can't wait to see her.
>
> We have so much to catch up on.
>
> Rose

For a long time Rosie stared ar her aunt's signature, fighting back the tears. Mom was grinning idiotically.

"Isn't it marvellous," she said, "And that's not the only

good news. Your Dad is coming home from Saudi. He arranged leave as soon as he heard what happened."

Rosie was thrilled. Dad home! Mom and Aunt Rose back together! An uncle she'd never seen and two cousins her own age, all arriving because of her.

But is it because of my trip to 1956 or because of my accident? she wondered. Maybe I imagined everything. Maybe Linda and Granda and Agnes Balfe and Miss Hackett were dreams. Yet they were so real!

Lost in her own reveries, Mom was startled when Rosie asked, "What happened to Miss Hackett?"

"Miss Hackett? Who's she?"

"Your teacher in fifth class. She gave Rose a terrible time. I read about it in her diary."

"Oh that Miss Hackett. Rose forgot her name too. As far as I remember she left at the end of the school year. There were rumours she was fired but we never found out. What an odd question!"

"And Agnes Balfe? What happened to her?"

"I haven't a clue. When we went to secondary school, she stayed on in Seventh Class. We never saw her again. Rosie, are you feeling alright?"

But her daughter was deep in concentration. She wanted to believe in her visit to the past. If it hadn't happened, if it was all in her imagination, then her mind was capable of rocketing out of control. She could be going mad. The brain was very delicate and its sudden encounter with a pavement would have done it no good at all.

From the look on her face Mom had doubts about her sanity too. Yet how could she remember Miss Hackett's classroom in such detail, down to the gold edging on the wings of those huge angels, if she hadn't been there. She took a deep breath, "Were there two statues in your class Mom?"

"Dear God you're raving! I tell you about Rose and

your Dad and you ask me about ancient history! Maybe I should call the doctor." But one look at Rosie's worried face made her answer. "Statues? Let me see . . . Yes there were. Enormous angels on either side of the blackboard. One was trying to squash a snake, a vicious looking creature – the angel, not the snake."

I'm not mad! Rosie thought, I didn't dream it. But then maybe Mom told me about them before and she's forgotten.

Something else occurred to her. "Where's my watch? If it's all a dream I should be wearing it."

Madge began to worry in earnest. "I'd best go and let you get some rest. Don't be worrying about your watch. I think it got smashed in the accident. The nurse would have thrown it out, but we can get you a new one."

After the visit, Rosie could not stop thinking. Her mind hopped from Agnes Balfe to Dad and whirled with angels and Miss Hackett. Shop bills and swings; letters and watches raced through her thoughts. What Mom feared happened. Her temperature ran high with fever and once more she lapsed into unconsciousness.

Again Madge spent a long anxious vigil at her side. Doctors and nurses came and went, barely whispering. Gran paid a brief visit and on the third day someone else arrived. Aunt Rose. She sat talking quietly to Madge and every so often directed her gaze at the figure in the bed as if willing her to get better. If she'd spoken or called her name, Rosie might have responded. Instead it was Uncle Jack who found the key to her subconscious.

He arrived early, on his way to work. "I called to see if there's anything I could do, Madge. Anything I can get you?"

She shook her head wearily.

"Well, at least let me take over for a while, even half an hour. You go and get some breakfast." Madge didn't want to, but Jack persuaded her. She needed to keep her strength up, he said. She'd be no good to Rosie if she collapsed would she? And if there was any change, why he'd buzz the doctor and run down to fetch her from the canteen.

When Madge had gone, Uncle Jack sat down beside Rosie, watching her closely. She was tossing and turning and every now and again would murmur feverishly. He bent to catch the words.

"No one would believe me. Hallucinations . . . h-a-l-l-u-c- . . . No one believes . . . " Jack held her hand and listened closely.

"Agnes Balfe . . . High Swing Challenge . . . " He felt his nerves tingle. Slowly he remembered a grey January day long ago and how he worried about his young sister's odd behaviour. He held his breath.

"Gave Jack the watch . . . He knew something was wrong . . . Changed the diary . . . Changed the past . . . The future . . . "

She was thrashing about in the bed, her face gleaming with sweat. Quickly Jack got up and went over to the wash stand. He wrung out a face cloth in cold water. Rosie was still rambling.

"No one could believe . . . hallucinations . . . " Suddenly she sat up, her eyes staring wildly, "No one! No one!"

Jack pushed her back on to the pillows and wiped her face with the damp cloth.

"It's all right Rosie," he said, "I believe you. It's me, Uncle Jack. I still have the watch."

Rosie stopped her fevered movements. Her mind seemed to be listening intently. Jack tried to choose his words carefully. He only vaguely remembered the watch his sister had given him. It had long ago stopped working and he had ceased to think of it. Now he realised why it had seemed so magical. It did not belong to 1956 at all. And it must have stopped when the tiny battery ran out. He was not sure what this was all about and that was why he proceeded so cautiously.

"I remember Rosie. I believe you. You gave the watch to me." Her face lost its anguished look and her breathing settled. Over and over he said soothingly. "You're not hallucinating. I believe you."

At last Rosie was completely calm. Soon she was sleeping peacefully. He buzzed for the doctor and went to tell Madge.

And instead of going to work that day, Jack paid a visit to Gran. "Remember that old diary Rose had when she was eleven? Did she throw it out, or take it with her or is it still here?"

Gran was astonished. "Funny you should mention that Jack. I'd quite forgotten it till Rosie went messing around in the attic the day before her accident. She found a few old things belonging to Madge and Rose – that diary among them. It's probably in her room."

Jack bounded up the stairs and into Rosie's bedroom. He found it in the top drawer. The faded inscription made him smile.

Rose O'Brien
Secret Diary
1956

Only a couple of weeks were filled in. Rose must have soon tired of it. He started reading, grinning broadly at the dreadful spelling. The first week took him back to that marvellous childhood Christmas – the snow woman, the slide, the Reillys – he even vaguely remembered the film and how much Rose had wanted to be Calamity Jane, borrowing his old holster and gun and firing at him every time he appeared. What wonderful days.

He noticed the change immediately he turned to Tuesday 10th January. Perfect spelling. Different handwriting. Freshly written – the words weren't faded at all for those last three days. Fascinated and tingling with excitement Jack read on. This was written by Rosie. Yet the events belonged to 1956 – the visit to the Royal, Miss Hackett, the fight with Agnes Balfe, the meeting at the shop etc. His heart almost stopped when he read the last entry:

Something awful may happen. Perhaps I won't be able to change a thing. Perhaps I won't get back to the 1990's.

Some strange experience had happened to Rosie when she was knocked down. And something strange had happened back in 1956. For a few days his young sister had behaved like someone else. What was it they had all laughed at? Oh yes . . . she'd said she wanted to be an engineer when she left school. It was so odd at the time. In those few days she seemed to have different ideas, almost a different set of values to the rest of them. And when she gave him the watch she was like a visitor from the future.

Was she from the future? Was it Rosie? Or had she just written up the diary the night before she was knocked down, using all the stories she'd heard plus her vivid imagination? Uncle Jack sighed. He was a practical scientific man by nature, an engineer by profession. His mind told him that what he felt had happened was just not possible. And yet . . .

In the hospital, Rosie remembered nothing about her uncle's visit. All she wanted now was to get well and she was determined to come to terms with her own doubts.

"Time travel is impossible," she concluded after much thought. "And anyway what does it matter if Aunt Rose and Mom are friends?"

Once she knew her aunt was home she had to see her. Madge wasn't at all keen.

"Now that you're conscious again the doctor doesn't want any visitors in case they upset you."

"I'll get more upset if she doesn't come," Rosie argued and added mischievously, "I promise, when she's here I won't show the slightest bit of interest."

"You're getting back to your old self right enough," Mom said dryly.

When her aunt arrived at last Rosie stared at her intently. She was still very like Mom – the same worry lines around the eyes, countered by an upturned humorous mouth. Just now she was smiling at Rosie who said the first daft thing that came into her head, "Mom thinks you're going to be a terrible strain and make me sick."

Rose looked astonished and Madge was horrified. Then her Aunt's eyes slowly crinkled and she began to laugh. The ice was broken.

Rosie wanted to know all about her aunt and her questions were answered just as eagerly. The family were staying in Dublin for at least a month, Rose said. The law firm could manage without her and Henry for that long and if things worked out the way she wanted . . . She stopped, afraid of running on about herself.

"Please," Mom said, "I want to know your plans and so does Rosie."

"Remember those dreams we had Madge? Of working together as lawyers?"

Mom nodded. "I'm afraid I lost interest in the law after you left."

"Well I want you to consider this proposition," Aunt Rose said. "Henry and I have discussed setting up a law firm here. We'd concentrate on legal work for American companies based in Ireland. If you went back to College and got your Law degree we'd keep a place for you and hope to expand the work to cover Irish businesses. What do you say?"

Mom said nothing. She was stunned. "It's not too late," her twin urged. "We could still be partners."

Rosie gave a nervous shout of laughter. "Mom can't be a student! She's not the right age and she's too . . . too . . . prim!"

Madge was outraged. "Let me tell you I can dress as badly as any student. You won't say prim when you see me with green hair and leggings. A ring in my nose and a bit of chewing gum and you won't be able to tell me apart from the rest."

Rosie blinked. People didn't put chewing gum up their noses. Flamin' hell! Aunt Rose was turning her mother into a middle-aged freak. And Madge had only begun to explore the possibilities!

"Maybe I'll be able to wear my old purple flairs and those red platform shoes I have at the back of the wardrobe . . . And that psychedelic yellow coat."

Help! Rosie was rapidly considering ways to get rid of Aunt Rose and her bad influence when she caught Mom's eye. She was grinning. So was Rose. The nerve! They were falling around the place, hysterical at Rosie's discomfort. She flung all the pillows at them, plus some grapes and tissues. A passing nurse, more used to a hushed silence surrounding this room, was drawn in by the shouts of laughter. She was promptly hit in the face by a pillow Rose had picked up and fired at Madge. The two culprits were more or less ordered out for disturbing the poor patient. They left under a cloud, still sniggering.

Chapter 15

"WELL YOU always wanted a Sinéad O'Connor haircut and now you've got one."

It was Sunday afternoon. Aunt Rose and her family were coming to tea and Rosie was home, minus the bandages. Mom was her conservative self again and looking rather doubtfully at her daughter's bald head.

"Your lovely long hair," she sighed, "I suppose they had to shave it off to operate."

"I think it's cool." Rosie was delighted, though she considered it a bit extreme that the haircut of her dreams took major surgery.

"Very cool," Madge said dryly, "especially with that purple stuff on the wound. You could be the leader of a skinhead gang except for the frilly nightdress."

Rosie grimaced. She hated the nightdress. Gran had bought it for her when she was in hospital, so she had to wear it. It was a pink satin affair with frills and bows. Rosie was sure Sinéad O'Connor wouldn't be seen dead in it.

"Could I get a leather jacket with studs for my next birthday?" she asked hopefully.

"No, you couldn't. Those Doc Martens are bad enough. Wearing them with that nightdress must be your notion of sartorial elegance."

Rosie caught the tone, though not the words. Dad had

given her the eighteen hole Docs as a "get well soon" present. She couldn't wait to wear them, even if they looked odd with the horrible nightdress. Mom had been really annoyed when Dad brought them home.

"Dear God, Frank, she won't look like a little girl at all. Now she'll never wear the nice woolly hat I bought to cover her baldness. You shouldn't encourage her!"

Rosie was indignant. "I'll wear no woolly hat. It's gross. I'd look like Compo from *The Last of the Summer Wine*. My bald head is lovely."

And Dad had added, "Madge, what does her hairstyle matter, or what she wears, once she's alive?" Mom had actually agreed – if a bit reluctantly.

It was wonderful having Dad home. As soon as he'd heard of her accident, he'd made the travel arrangements. Not only that, he'd got a permanent transfer to his company's office in Dublin. "It means less income, Rosie," he'd said, hugging her, "and maybe a step down the ladder, but no amount of money or success can make up for home. I won't be going away again."

And Mom had made up her mind to do the Law degree, once she and Dad agreed they could afford it.

Life had changed alright. Of course Gran still took a nap on Sunday afternoons and Mom's table was still piled high with school work. Soon it would be law books instead of copies.

"Why don't you like teaching?" Rosie asked her.

"Oh, because it isn't what I originally wanted and because I hate all the corrections and don't have the patience for dealing with youngsters. Teaching makes me very cross, though I hope I'm not as bad as Miss Hackett."

"You couldn't be!" Rosie said with utter conviction.

She looked once more at the locket around her neck. Aunt Rose had told her she could keep it. In an odd way it comforted her. For the face was very like her own and there was no green ribbon on the left plait. The small face smiled reassuringly as if to say, "I'll succeed. I'll help."

While Mom was putting away her papers and preparing for the arrival of the visitors, Uncle Jack arrived. "I just called to give you this, Rosie." He opened his hand. Her watch! She said nothing. He gazed at her steadily and then grinned. "It gave us a powerful victory over Agnes Balfe, didn't it!" Rosie gasped. He knew! Uncle Jack knew what had happened! So it wasn't a dream or hallucination.

"You know, Rosie, I hadn't thought about that watch for years. To all intents and purposes I'd forgotten it. Then when you were sick you mentioned it and afterwards everything came flooding back, fresh as yesterday."

He paused, a faraway look in his eyes. "The day I took the watch into class was one of the best days of my life. The fellas were fascinated! The teacher couldn't get over it. It was like I'd produced something really magic. A new invention or discovery not yet dreamed of. Not in Dublin in the fifties anyway." He smiled as he remembered.

"The teacher called in the headmaster and everyone crowded around, testing more and more complicated sums, trying out the memory and the alarm. The headmaster talked about the marvels of modern science. That was when I knew, Rosie, what I wanted to do with my future, electronic engineering, though I didn't know the name then."

Rosie was overawed to realise how much her brief visit to the past had influenced so many lives.

"What do you think happened to me, Uncle Jack ?" she whispered. "How did I get back to the past?"

"I don't really know Rosie. Perhaps it was some sort of will power on your part. Single minded determination has won a lot of battles for people, against difficulties like sickness and danger. Maybe you had that kind of determination. And maybe the sudden blow to your head cleared some sort of route to the past. But I'm only guessing Rosie, and probably not too well."

They lapsed into silence for a few moments then Uncle Jack continued, "Anyway, better to keep our knowledge to ourselves for the moment. Your Aunt Rose doesn't know what happened."

He smiled. "And by the way, your watch needs a new battery. It stopped on me after a year. I never knew what was up with it!"

Just then Gran came down from her nap and Dad came in from his walk. Uncle Jack couldn't stay for dinner and left soon afterwards. The table was set for the visitors. They were coming at five o'clock.

As the hour approached Rosie's heart began to beat faster with anticipation. She kept watch out the window and soon she saw them – Aunt Rose with a tall man and two children about her own age walking up the road. Well . . . three of them were walking. The boy was dancing around the others pounding his chest. They paid no attention. Undaunted he raced ahead and jumped for the branch of a tree and began to swing out of it.

The girl was tall and dark and seemed very sedate. Then suddenly she made a run at the boy and tickled his waist. He shrieked and collapsed in a heap. She raced away and he followed at speed. A wrestling match took place at the gate. Aunt Rose and Uncle Henry calmly stepped around the writhing bodies and rang the doorbell.

Her cousins tumbled into the room, out of breath.

"Hi Rosie," they chorused, looking entirely dishevelled. The boy Shane bounded over to her, punching the air around her with playful jabs. "Cool hair Rosie." Dooh – dooh – dooh went his fists. His sister Hattie shoved him out of the way. He socked her on the nose. Not very hard. She kicked his shin. "Oww! You can't do that to Mike the Tyke Tyson!"

Uncle Jack all over again! Rosie's heart lifted even higher. Hattie sat down beside her.

"It's neat you're my cousin Rosie. I sure need a change from Swinging Shane here! He's a looper. Totally out of it. Wired to the Moon." Rosie smiled to herself. Shane was still bouncing around.

"You gotta ignore her Rosie. She wants to be a Sumo wrestler. With a body weight of eighty pounds – I ask you ! Hattie the Hornet more like." The girls began to giggle.

Aunt Rose was staring at the watch still clutched in Rosie's hand. "Can I see that?" She examined it closely, her eyes narrowing in an effort to remember. "It's a bit like the one I found in O'Connell Street, years ago. Do you recall, Madge?"

Madge didn't.

"Well I do. And maybe Jack does. I think I gave it to him. He was so taken by it. We took ages to work out everything it could do and we thought it was a marvel, though it probably wasn't half as complicated as this one. I don't know why yours in particular reminded me." She frowned, then handing back the watch she shrugged her shoulders, dismissing the memory.

Rosie sighed. She was never going to know if her trip to 1956 was real.

"I guess those two are a tonic for Rosie," Uncle Henry said, "though I reckon with us renting a house around the corner we are going to have one big problem." He paused while the others waited apprehensively. "Can't you see it?" he asked, waving a hand at the cousins. "When these guys get together it'll be Chaos Time." He shook his head gloomily, though Rosie detected the glint of laughter in his eyes. "The Terrible Trio means Mega Trouble." There was a collective groan from the adults.

But for Rosie, the words struck an instant glorious chord. How wonderful to be part of a Terrible Trio! No more dreadful Sunday afternoons.

Soon she heard Dad ask Uncle Henry about American football and looked over to where Aunt Rose and Mom were chatting with Gran. Everyone was absorbed and happy.

It was time to let go of the past.

The future was waiting impatiently for The Terrible Trio – waiting with its great unknown adventures.

"Massive!"

THE END

Also by Poolbeg

The Hiring Fair

by

Elizabeth O'Hara

It is 1890 and Parnell is the uncrowned king of Ireland. But thirteen-year-old Sally Gallagher, "Scatterbrain Sally" as her mother and younger sister Katie call her, has no interest in politics. She is happy to read books and leave the running of the house to those who like housework.

A shocking tragedy changes the lives of the sisters. Instead of being the daughters of a comfortable Donegal farmer and fisherman, they have to become hired servants, bound for six months to masters they don't know.

Elizabeth O'Hara has written an exciting story that has its share of sorrow and joy. She creates in Scatterbrain Sally a new and unforgettable Irish heroine.

Also by Poolbeg

The Sequel to *The Hiring Fair*

Blaeberry Sunday

by

Elizabeth O'Hara

That summer had changed the course of her life for ever: "Was every little thing that happened as significant as every other little thing in shaping the course of a person's life?"

The summer leading up to Blaeberry Sunday – the festival of Lughnasa – in 1893 was the hottest and driest anyone in Donegal had ever experienced.

Determined not to remain a hired girl for the rest of her days, Sally returns to glenbra only to witness an eviction, death, and the courtship of her mother and Packy Doherty, a local farmer.

Nothing, however, is quite so devastating as her love for Manus McLoughlin and the events preceding that fateful Blaeberry Sunday.